W9-BLR-164

The Anne of Green Gables Christmas Treasury

The Anne of Green Gables Christmas Treasury

CAROLYN STROM COLLINS

CHRISTINA WYSS ERIKSSON

VIKING

Viking
Published by the Penguin Group
Penguin Books Canada Ltd, 10 Alcorn Avenue, Toronto, Ontario, Canada M4V 3B2
Penguin Books Ltd, 27 Wrights Lane, London W8 5TZ, England
Viking Penguin, a division of Penguin Books USA Inc., 375 Hudson Street, New York, New York 10014, U.S.A.
Penguin Books Australia Ltd, Ringwood, Victoria, Australia
Penguin Books (NZ) Ltd, Cnr Rosedale and Airborne Roads, Albany, Auckland 1310, New Zealand
Penguin Books Ltd, Registered Offices: Harmondsworth, Middlesex, England

First published 1997
1 3 5 7 9 10 8 6 4 2

Printed and bound in England on acid free paper

Canadian Cataloguing in Publication Data
Collins, Carolyn
The Anne of Green Gables Christmas treasury
ISBN 0-670-87031-5
1. Montgomery, L. M. (Lucy Maud), 1876–1942. Anne of Green Gables. 2. Christmas - Prince Edward Island. 3. Christmas decorations. 4. Christmas cookery. 5. Handicraft. I. Eriksson, Christina Wyss. II. Montgomery, L. M. (Lucy Maud), 1876-1942. Anne of Green Gables. III. Title.
PS8526.055A776 1997 C813'.52 C96-930085-9
PR9199.2.M65A776 1997

American Library of Congress Cataloguing in Publication Data Available

---

Visit Penguin Canada's web site at **www.penguin.ca**

CONTENTS

Introduction

Green Gables had a very festal appearance as they drove up the lane. There was a light in every window, the glow breaking out through the darkness like flame-red blossoms swung against the dark background of the Haunted Wood.

ANNE OF THE ISLAND, VII

Before Anne Shirley arrived one fine June day, Green Gables was a rather lacklustre old farmhouse with only the elderly Matthew and Marilla Cuthbert left to care for it. Eleven-year-old Anne, an orphan from Nova Scotia, was sent to the Cuthberts "by mistake" — they had requested a boy from the orphanage to come to Green Gables in order to help Matthew with the heavy farm chores — but the mistake turned out to be the most fortunate thing that ever happened to Matthew, Marilla, Green Gables and Avonlea! She was an irrepressible, unpredictable, irresistable redhead with seven freckles and an imagination that never seemed to run out.

Like so many other changes that "crept in" over the years at Green Gables after Anne came to live there, Christmas began to be celebrated again. Anne's first Christmas at Green Gables is not even mentioned in *Anne of Green Gables,* and we must assume it was uneventful. Anne's second Christmas, as described in *Anne of Green Gables,* however, is one of the most memorable scenes in all the Anne books, for it is the Christmas that Matthew presents Anne with her first puff-sleeved dress. Beaded slippers from Miss Josephine Barry and a festive concert at the Avonlea Hall combine to make this Christmas unforgettable, for Anne as well as for her "kindred spirits."

We learn that Anne always went home to Green Gables for Christmas, whether she was at Queen's College in Charlottetown, Redmond University in Kingsport, or teaching at Summerside High School, and before the train left the station, she "was already tasting Christmas happiness," looking forward to the "hugs and exclamations and laughter" that would surround her when she opened the door, the same kitchen door she first entered with Matthew on her arrival at Green Gables.

Other memorable Christmases from the Anne books include Katherine Brooke's reluctant visit to Green Gables (*Anne of Windy Poplars*), Anne and Gilbert's first Christmas together at Four Winds Point (*Anne's House of Dreams*) and Aunt Mary Maria's Christmas visit to Ingleside (*Anne of Ingleside*). These few glimpses of Christmases with Anne through the years provide us with some idea of what a Green Gables Christmas might have been like once Anne had infused it with her special touch — the gifts exchanged, the seasonal decorations, the Christmas tree, the festive clothing, the kinds of entertainment and the special feasts and treats that Anne enjoyed at Christmastime.

In *The Anne of Green Gables Christmas Treasury* you will find many ways to make some of the Green Gables holiday customs part of your own tradition — decorating with fresh evergreens and other natural materials as Anne and Katherine did; making gifts for your own "kindred spirits"; fashioning your own Christmas tree ornaments in the Victorian style of Anne's day; stitching up a few items

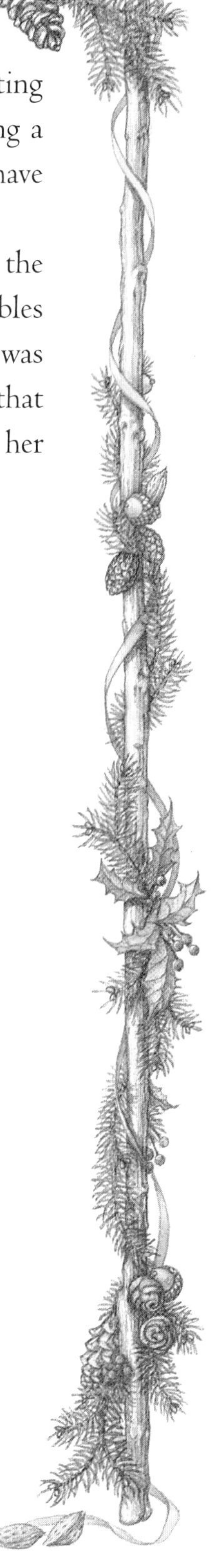

of clothing and accessories that would have suited Anne and Diana; inviting friends for a special "Christmas Concert," Avonlea-style; and even preparing a Christmas dinner with many of the same foods Anne and Marilla would have served.

Some of the activities included in this book did not actually appear in the Anne books but are inspired by them, such as the making of the Green Gables Gingerbread House and the Green Gables Tea Cosy. But we know that there was often gingerbread in the pantry and a pot of tea at every meal, so we hope that these additions to Anne's Green Gables Christmas celebrations meet with her approval — and yours!

C. S.C. and C.W. E.

Green Gables Decorations

"Oh, look, there's one little early wild rose out! Isn't it lovely? Don't you think it must be glad to be a rose? Wouldn't it be nice if roses could talk? I'm sure they could tell us such lovely things. And isn't pink the most bewitching colour in the world?"

ANNE OF GREEN GABLES, V

The wild rose that Anne noticed as she and Marilla drove down the Green Gables lane on Anne's first morning at Green Gables was blooming in June, of course, not December. Nevertheless, it tells us right away of Anne's love of roses that lasted all her life. Roses are prominently featured throughout the Anne books, in gardens, on windowsills — Anne and Marilla cultivated "house roses" that bloomed in Green Gables' sunny windows year 'round — in bouquets, scattered on tablecloths at tea time, even intertwined with buttercups around the brim of Anne's hat one Sunday! Both Anne and her bosom friend, Diana, carried roses in their wedding bouquets.

Planning a Green Gables Christmas around a rose theme is the ideal way to celebrate Christmas with Anne and her "kindred spirits" in mind. Not only do you celebrate Anne's love of roses, you can bring in other elements of the late-Victorian-style Christmas, as well, with plenty of fancy ribbons, lace, doilies, velvet, tapestry and many other elegant materials.

Since the Christmas tree is likely to be the focal point of your holiday decorating, let's begin with it.

Anne's Wild-Rose Christmas Tree With Handmade Decorations

Queen Victoria, who was Queen of England from 1837 to 1901, is credited with making the Christmas tree a popular addition to today's Christmas celebrations. Her husband, Prince Albert, introduced her to the German custom early in their marriage. Once the Queen and her family started having Christmas trees in their home for the holidays, other people wanted to have them, too. At first, communities would have one tree in a central location, perhaps in a church or the town hall, where people would come to see it on Christmas Day and have a party around the decorated tree. Later, families began to have their own trees at home, usually decorated on Christmas Eve after the children had gone to bed, for a stunning Christmas morning surprise.

The first time we are told of a Christmas tree at Green Gables is in *Anne of Windy Poplars*. The year would have been 1889.

> *The plum pudding was concocted and the Christmas tree brought home. Katherine and Anne and Davy and Dora went to the woods for it . . . a beautiful little fir to whose cutting down Anne was only reconciled by the fact that it was in a little clearing of Mr. Harrison's which was going to be stumped and plowed in the spring anyhow.*

For Anne's Wild-Rose Christmas Tree, decorate the tree with tissue roses, lacy cones, fan ornaments, ribbon garlands, rose-hip wreaths and tiny white lights — all popular decorations in the Victorian era.

Put the lights on the tree first. In Anne's day, tiny candles were attached to the tree and lit just before the tree was displayed. Now, of course, we use strings of electric lights. Tiny white lights will simulate nicely the candles Anne would have used.

And now for the decorations!

Pink and White Tissue Roses

At the Christmas concert in Avonlea Hall, to which Anne wore her first puff-sleeved dress and beaded slippers from Mrs. Josephine Barry, the decorations were fashioned from evergreens and "pink tissue paper roses" and Anne wore a "wreath of white roses" on her hair. You may also remember that Gilbert Blythe was observed picking up one of the roses that fell from Anne's hair and slipping it into his pocket. Make as many of these tissue roses as you can, for they are the basis of your Wild-Rose Christmas. You can use them not only on your Christmas tree, but also on wreaths and garlands, as gift-package decorations, in centrepieces and in many other ways.

You will need:

Pink gift-wrap tissue

White gift-wrap tissue

Green florist's tape

Fine florist's wire

Scissors

Wire snips

1 For each tissue rose, cut a piece of tissue, at least 20 inches (50 cm) long into a strip measuring 6 inches (15 cm) at one end and 4 inches (10 cm) at the other. Fold it in half lengthwise so that you have a doubled 20-inch (50-cm) piece of tissue that is 3 inches (7.5 cm) wide on one end and 2 inches (5 cm) at the other. Crumple the tissue slightly to soften it and to create more realistic-looking petals.

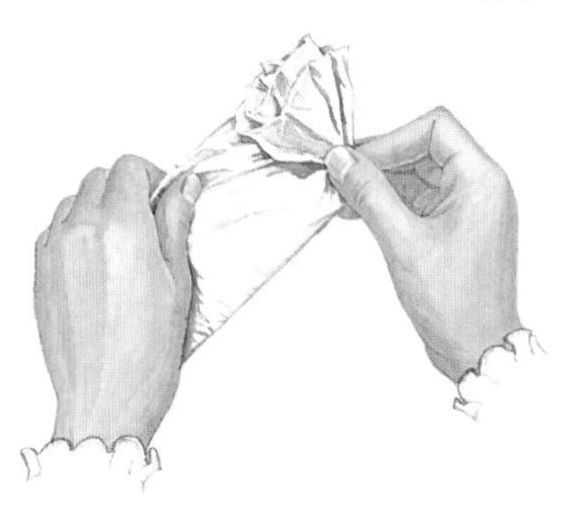

2 Starting at the end that is 2 inches (5 cm) wide (with the folded edge along the bottom), fold the top corner down and begin to roll the tissue over several times into a tight "bud." Gather and roll the tissue, pinching it firmly at the bottom and flaring it slightly wider with each turn until you have a rose. This may take a few practice tries, but it will not hurt the rose to start over several times.

3 Turn down the top edge of the tissue a little in several places to add a more realistic look.

4 Bind the bottom ½ inch (12 mm) of the rose with green florist's tape, then attach a piece of fine florist's wire and continue to tape around it to make a "stem." Cut the wire with wire cutters or heavy-duty scissors that are made to cut fine wire and other hard materials. Do not use your fabric scissors or good paper scissors on wire!

Christmas Rose Bouquets

A few tissue roses clustered into bouquets can be set among the branches of your Christmas tree.

For each bouquet, you will need:

---

3 or 4 tissue roses *(see page 6)*

1 round paper lace doily (optional), 6 to 8 inches (15 to 20 cm) in diameter

12 inches (30 cm) green satin, velvet, grosgrain or paper ribbon

---

1 Gather several tissue roses into a bunch and twist the wire stems together. If desired, cut a small hole in a paper doily, slip the stems of the bouquet into it and push the doily up close to the blossoms.

2 Tie a coordinating length of ribbon in a bow around the stems of the bouquet. Set the bouquet among the branches of your tree; twist the wire stem around the branch to hold the bouquet in place.

Miniature Rose Bouquets

You can purchase packages of tiny silk rosebuds on stems at fabric stores and bridal supply shops. Cluster six or seven of the rosebuds in the same colour or mixed colours (for the Anne tree, we recommend white, pink and/or burgundy roses) and wire them together. Tie a matching narrow satin or grosgrain ribbon around the cluster. These miniature bouquets, used with the larger tissue roses or by themselves, are charming accents on the Christmas tree. They also make attractive package decorations.

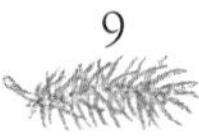

Lacy Paper Cones

Paper cones were popular in Victorian times for holding candy, flowers and other delights. Roses and lace go together so beautifully; these lacy cones will look just right on your Wild-Rose Christmas Tree.

1 round paper lace doily (white or gold), 6 to 8 inches (15 to 20 cm) in diameter

Tape, glue or sticker

Scissors

8-inch (20-cm) length of ¼-inch (6-mm) pink, white, green or burgundy satin ribbon

Tissue

Potpourri, tissue rose or Christmas candies

1 Choose a size of doily that will be best for your tree. The smaller the tree, the smaller the doily you will use. Roll the doily into a cone shape, pointed at the bottom and open at the top. Tape or glue the cone closed (or use a pretty sticker to secure the edge of the cone, if you prefer).

2 Cut a small slit in each side, about ½ inch (12 mm) from the top edge. Put one end of the ribbon through one slit, the other end through the other slit. Knot the ends.

3 Crumple some tissue and fill the bottom third of the cone to provide a base. Add a small handful of potpourri, a tissue rose (see page 6), a miniature rose bouquet (see page 9) or some candies to peek out of the top of the cone. (These paper cones are delicate and cannot hold much weight, so keep the "filling" light.) Make as many cones as you like and hang them on the tree.

Lacy Paper Fans

Fans were a popular accessory for Victorian ladies. They were made of many different materials—paper, bamboo, silk, ivory, lace, even feathers. Wouldn't Anne have loved to put these little lacy fans on her Christmas tree?

For each fan, you will need:

1 round paper lace doily, 6 to 8 inches (15 to 20 cm) in diameter

Embroidery or darning needle

Fine florist's wire

Wire snips

3-inch (7.5-cm) tassel

1 Fold the doily in half. Accordion-pleat the semi-circle to make a fan shape.

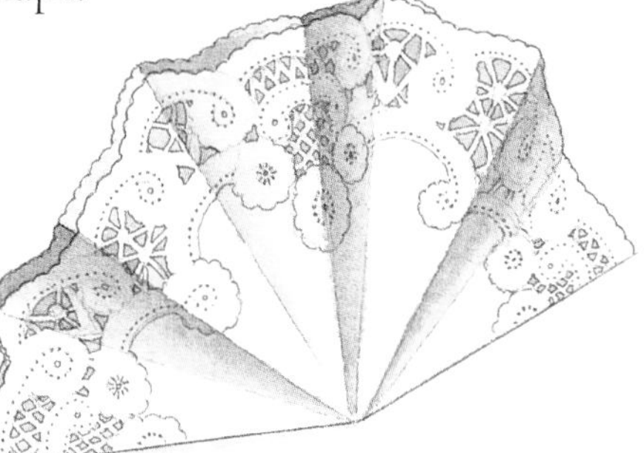

2 One-half inch (12 mm) from the bottom, run the needle through the pleats. Place a 3-inch (7.5-cm) length of florist's wire through the hole

and slip the tassel onto the wire. Twist the wire firmly to hold the tassel in place. Snip off the ends of the wire.

3 Spread out the pleats of the fan and place the fan on the tree. Make as many as you like.

"Kindred Spirits" Hand-and-Heart Ornaments

"We must join hands—so," said Anne gravely. "It ought to be over running water." Always on the watch for "kindred spirits," Anne knew immediately when she met Diana at Orchard Slope that they would be friends. Anne, of course, suggested that they clasp hands across the garden path (there being no running water nearby) and swear to be faithful bosom friends "as long as the sun and moon shall endure."

These dainty hand ornaments, a popular motif in the Victorian era, will be a beautiful reminder of Anne and Diana's "solemn vow and promise."

For one ornament, you will need:

1 white index card or other lightweight cardboard, 5 by 7 inches (13 by 18 cm)

1 white paper lace doily, 4 by 6 inches (10 by 15 cm) or any scrap of lace, 4 by 6 inches (10 by 15 cm)

4-inch (10-cm) length of 1-inch (2.5-cm) wide white lace with ribbon insert

8-inch (20-cm) length ¼-inch (6-mm) wide matching satin ribbon

Pencil

Scissors

Glue

¼-inch (6-mm) coloured or pearl heart-shaped button (optional)

1 Outline your hand, fingers and thumb close together, with pencil on the white card. You may need to reduce the size of the drawing slightly so that you have an outline about 6 inches (15 cm) long and 4 inches (10 cm) wide. Include 1 inch (2.5 cm) or so at the bottom for the wrist.

2 Cut out the hand shape. Glue the paper doily or lace scrap on top and trim it to fit. Glue the lace edging around the wrist with the seam on the back. Glue the two ends of the ribbon to the back, about ½ inch (12 mm) from the edge of the wrist, to make a loop.

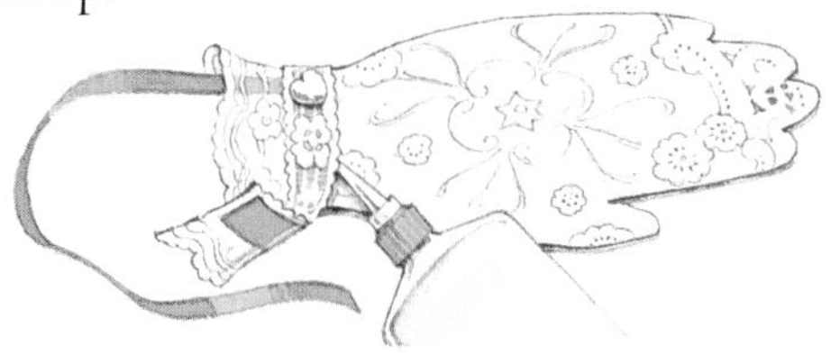

3 Sew a small coloured or pearl heart-shaped button to the lace cuff, if desired.

4 Hang as many of these ornaments on the Christmas tree as you like. They can also be used as placecards, gift tags or bookmarks.

Wreaths of Roseberries

Anne and Diana made "necklaces of roseberries" in "Idlewild," the playhouse they had created in a "little ring of white birches" near Green Gables. Why not make "wreaths of roseberries" for your Wild-Rose Christmas Tree? Anne's rose-berries were probably rose-hips, the tiny fruits of the wild roses that grew along the lane leading to Green Gables. Rose-hips can be harvested in the fall. You can use dried rosebuds, if you prefer, or fresh cranberries.

Rose-hips and dried rosebuds are available at florist and craft shops.

For one wreath, you will need:

12 to 18 rose-hips (or dried rosebuds)

12 to 18 inches (30 to 45 cm) fine florist's wire

Wire snips

8-inch (20-cm) length of 1/4-inch (6-mm) narrow satin ribbon in white, pink, burgundy or green

1 If you have a small tree, use the smaller quantities and measurements for your wreath. For an average- to large-size tree, use the larger quantities and measurements.

2 Thread the rose-hips or rosebuds onto the florist wire, leaving about 2 inches (5 cm) of wire uncovered at each end. When you have all the rose-hips on the wire, shape it into a circle. Twist the ends of the wire together and clip off the excess. Tie a ribbon in a bow at the top of the wreath, trim the ends to the length you want, and hang the wreath on the tree. Make as many wreaths as you like.

A Necklace of Roseberries

You might also want to make a "necklace of roseberries" as a gift for a friend — just use a needle and heavy thread to string the rose-hips and make the necklace long enough to slip over the head, about 28 inches (70 cm) long. Tie the ends of the thread securely.

Ribbon Garlands and Ribbon Chains

Ribbon garlands and ribbon chains were popular Christmas tree decorations in Victorian times, as they are still. For a sumptuous look to your Wild-Rose Tree, thread ribbon garlands or ribbon chains through the branches.

Ribbon Garlands

6 to 12 6-foot (1.8-metre) lengths of pink, white or burgundy velvet ribbon, 1 to 2 inches (2.5 to 5 cm) wide

Scissors

1 Cut the ends of the ribbon into points.

2 Weave the velvet ribbons, one at a time, through the branches of the Christmas tree, starting at the top and working your way around the tree to the bottom.

Ribbon Chains

If you prefer, decorate your tree with colourful ribbon chains.

¼-inch (5-mm) wide ribbon in several colours, cut into 6-inch (15-cm) lengths (You will need at least 24 lengths for a 6-foot/1.8-metre chain.)

Scissors

Tape or glue

1 Choose colours of ribbon that will coordinate with the other colours on your tree — pink, white, burgundy, green, gold, silver and patterned ribbon in those colours. Satin, velvet and grosgrain ribbon scraps as well as shiny paper ribbon or strips of coloured paper can be used.

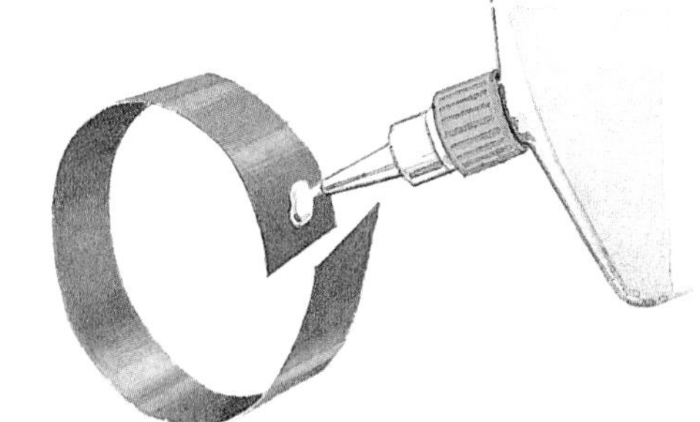

2 Loop one ribbon strip (right side out) into a circle, overlapping the ends by about ½ inch (12 mm). Tape or glue into place. Insert another strip through the circle, and tape the ends. Repeat until you have a long length of ribbon chain to loop around the tree.

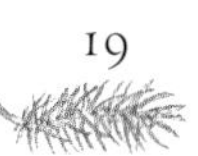

Wild-Rose Christmas Tree Topper

In Anne of Ingleside, *we learn that Anne and Gilbert set a silver star atop their Christmas tree, and you may want to find one for your own tree, as well. Or make up a nosegay of tissue roses, tie it with streamers of pretty ribbon and attach it to the top of your tree with wire.*

Lacy Christmas Tree Skirt

Handmade lace was used in many ways at Green Gables. Handkerchiefs and petticoats were edged in narrow lace, pillowcases and sheets in luxuriously wide lace. On the black horsehair furniture in the parlour there were Marilla's crocheted "white antimacassars that were always laid at a perfectly correct angle, except at such times as they clung to unfortunate people's buttons." Large tablecloths and bedspreads were made entirely of lace and stiff lace curtains hung over the parlour windows. Anne and Marilla turned out yards and yards of knitted or crocheted lace while they sat by the Waterloo stove on winter evenings or on the bench by the front door in summer.

A pretty piece of lace or lace-edged fabric would be ideal for covering the tree stand of your Wild-Rose Christmas Tree. Simply drape an inexpensive lacy tablecloth or even a lacy window curtain panel around the base of your tree to complete the romantic theme.

Evergreen Parlour Decorations

In *Anne of Windy Poplars,* Anne plunges into decorating Green Gables when she comes home for the Christmas holiday. She has been living in Summerside, presiding over the high school and trying to make friends with a fellow teacher, the sour and disagreeable Katherine Brooke. She invites Katherine to spend Christmas at Green Gables, in hopes that Katherine will see a happier side of life than she has known before.

Anne and Katherine roam the woods around Green Gables, gathering armloads of evergreen boughs and other materials for decorating the old farmhouse, especially the parlour, that "rather severe and gloomy apartment" that Marilla reserved for special occasions.

Anne & Katherine's Christmas Wreaths

Anne and Katherine Brooke "wandered about, gathering creeping spruce and ground pine for wreaths" and "even some ferns that kept green in a certain deep hollow of the woods all winter." Then they fashioned the greenery into wreaths and swags to hang on the doors, in the windows or over the mantels.

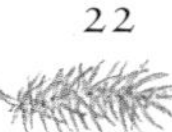

To make a fresh evergreen wreath for your front door or to hang over the fireplace mantel, you will need:

Evergreen branches (spruce, pine, cedar, fir and other greens available at florists and nurseries at holiday time); gather your own only if you own the property on which the evergreens are growing!

Wire wreath frame, about 15 inches (38 cm) in diameter

Fine florist's wire

Heavy-duty scissors for cutting the branches

Wire snips

4 yards (3.6 m) of wide (2- to 4-inch/ 5- to 10-cm) pink, red or burgundy velvet ribbon

Tissue roses (optional) *(see page 6)*

1 Cut the greens into pieces 6 to 8 inches (15 to 20 cm) long. Bunch several pieces together and wrap the stems with fine wire to hold them securely. Make several dozen of these bundles; as you make them, arrange them on the wire wreath frame just to keep track of how many bundles you need to make.

2 Wire the bundles of greens onto the frame, one at a time, by winding the wire over the stem ends and around the wire of the frame. Lay succeeding bundles so that their greenery covers the stems and wire of the previous bundle. Lay all the bundles in the same direction. Cover the frame thickly.

3 Tie a large ribbon bow at the top or at the bottom of the wreath and hang it up on a nail or a hook. (If your wreath frame does not have a built-in hanging loop, make one out of several thicknesses of the wrapping wire and twist the ends onto the frame.)

4 You may wish to wire tissue roses onto the wreath if it is going to hang in the room with your Wild-Rose Christmas Tree (but not on a door that is exposed to the elements — the tissue roses will wilt). Or if you have collected small branches with rose-hips, berries or cones on them, dried grasses, ferns or other natural materials, you could add them to your wreath.

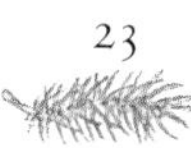

Ingleside Window Wreaths

Ingleside was Anne and Gilbert's home in Glen St. Mary. Anne liked to hang a small evergreen wreath in each window at Christmastime.

1 To make your own window wreaths, wire small bunches of evergreen to 8-inch (20-cm) wire wreath frames just as you did for the larger wreath on page 22. Hang one wreath by a ribbon loop at the centre of as many windows as you like, perhaps each window on the front of your house.

2 To determine how much ribbon you will need, measure from the top of the window to the level you wish to hang the wreath; double the measurement and add about 24 inches (60 cm) to allow for a bow. Multiply this length by the number of window wreaths you plan to use.

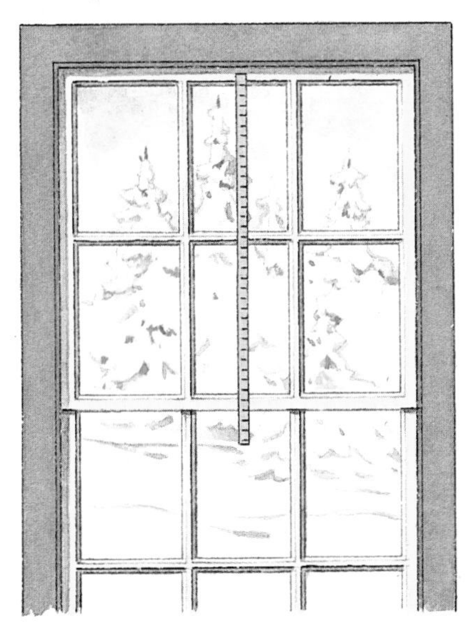

3 Tie a length of 1½- to 2-inch (4- to 5-cm) ribbon through the wreath and tie the ends in a bow. Hang the ribbon on a small nail in the middle of the top of each window frame or loop the ribbon around the drapery rod and tie it in a bow. The bow can remain at the top of the window or you can bring it down so that it rests at the top of the wreath.

Other Evergreen Decorations

Evergreen decorations can be used throughout the house. Here are some suggestions, but use your imagination to create your own festive touches.

1 Instead of wreaths, you can make "swags." Gather several branches of evergreen together, tie the stems with fine wire, then wrap with ribbon. Hang a large swag on the door and smaller ones in the windows.

2 Lay small branches of evergreen on windowsills, mantels or down the centre of a table; decorate with tissue roses, lacy fan ornaments, ribbons, etc., if you wish.

3 Place holly or evergreen sprigs at the tops of pictures and mirrors, a popular Victorian Christmas custom.

4 Make garlands of evergreen (wire bundles of evergreen together just as you did for the wreath, page 22, then wire them into long ropes) to wind around stair banisters and newel posts, or to edge doorways and windowsills outside.

5 Fill a large pot about halfway with soil or gravel and arrange branches of evergreen in the pot. Set the arrangement on your front porch.

6 Place vases filled with evergreen branches on tables throughout the house; add a few stems of roses or carnations and tie ribbons around the vases for an extra-festive look. Set the vases on crocheted doilies or other mats to protect tabletops.

7 Fill a bowl with shiny red apples (russets were Anne's favourite and there were always plenty of them picked from the Green Gables orchard in the fall and stored in the cellar for the winter); slip sprigs of evergreen amongst the apples. Set the bowl on a table or on a hearth for a festive and edible accent.

8 Surround a punchbowl with evergreen branches.

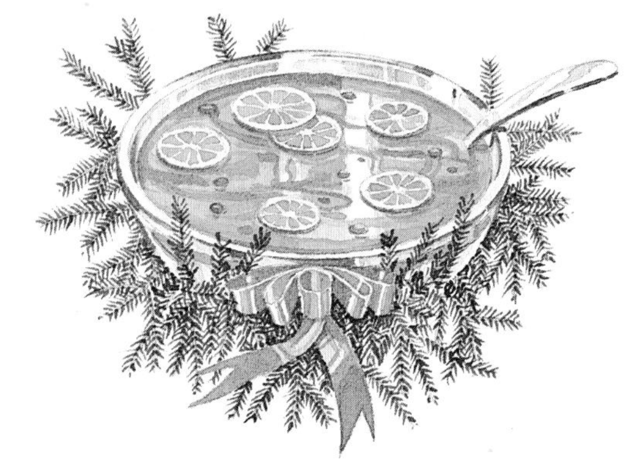

9 Tie tiny sprigs of evergreen into the bows on the tops of wrapped gifts.

Tasselled Mistletoe Ball

Another very popular Victorian custom that we still see today was the mistletoe ball. Mistletoe grows in the tops of trees and is brought down at Christmastime to add to the festive atmosphere. Anyone caught standing under a sprig of mistletoe is considered a candidate for a kiss!

To make a mistletoe ball, you will need:

1 small (2- to 3-inch/5- to 7.5-cm) apple (or styrofoam ball)

Several sprigs of mistletoe (This can be bought in florist shops at holiday time.)

Several sprigs of other evergreen such as spruce, cedar, fir, pine, boxwood or holly

1 to 2 yards (1 to 2 metres) 1/4-inch (5-mm) satin or velvet ribbon

Scissors

Pins

Metal skewer or nail

1 tassel to match the ribbon (optional), 3 to 4 inches (7.5 to 10 cm) long

1 Tie the ribbon around the apple as shown, leaving two ends of 12 inches (30 cm) or more for a hanging loop; pin the ribbon into place.

2 Cut the mistletoe and evergreen into small sprigs, about 1 to 2 inches (2.5 to 5 cm) long. Poke holes all over the apple with the skewer or nail and insert the greenery into the holes so that the apple is completely covered. The mistletoe can be mixed randomly with the other greens or clustered in one spot at the bottom of the ball.

3 Pin the tassel to the bottom of the ball where the ribbon criss-crosses itself. Hang the mistletoe ball in the centre of a doorway or from a light fixture in your front entrance hall or wherever you like.

4 The moisture in the apple will help keep the greenery fresh. You may also want to spritz the mistletoe ball with a light mist of water every day or two, as well.

Tapestry Christmas Table Runner

Tapestry, a richly woven heavy fabric, was a favourite material of the Victorians. It was used most often for draperies and upholstery. A beautiful holiday table runner can be made from tapestry. Choose colours that will coordinate with your Christmas decorations.

For a 12-inch (30-cm) wide, 52-inch (130-cm) long runner, you will need:

3/8 yard (34 cm) medium-weight tapestry fabric, 52 inches (130 cm) wide

3/8 yard (34 cm) cotton fabric, 52 inches (130 cm) wide

Matching thread

Needle and pins

Scissors

2 tassels (optional)

---

1 Pin the tapestry and cotton fabrics right sides together. Trim edges to match.

2 Hem around three sides of the fabric, about 3/8 inch (9 mm) from the edges. Clip the corners and turn the piece inside out. Turn the open edges under 3/8 inch (9 mm), press them flat with a warm iron, and hand-sew the opening closed. Press around all four sides of the runner so that the edges are sharp and flat.

3 Place the runner down the middle of your dining table.

4 If you wish, you can make a longer runner which hangs over the ends of the table. Measure the table on which you wish to use the runner and add 1 yard (1 metre) to the measurement. If your table is longer than the fabric, stitch two or more lengths of tapestry together. Do the same with the lining. Sew the lining to the tapestry and finish the runner as directed above.

5 Fold the ends into points, tack them to the lining, and press flat. Sew a tassel onto each point. Place the runner down the centre of the table with the ends overhanging the table about 18 inches (45 cm) on each end.

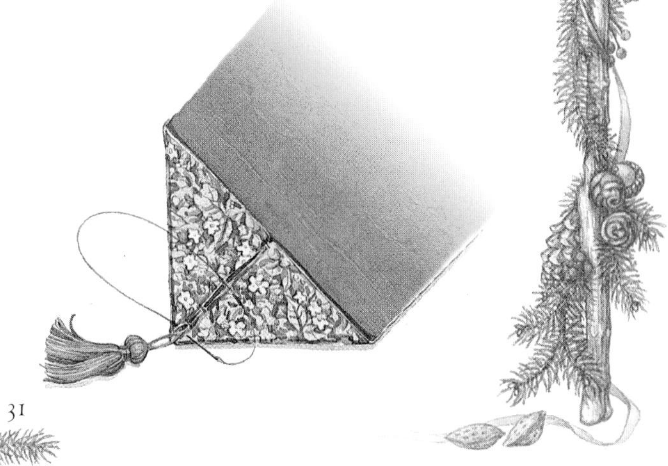

A Green Gables Gingerbread House

Making a gingerbread house has been a delightful Christmas custom for many years. Everyone knows the story of Hansel and Gretel and their encounter with the old witch who lived in a gingerbread house deep in the forest.

You can make a gingerbread house that looks just like the very Green Gables that Anne loved to go home to at Christmas. This is how she described Green Gables to her college chum Phillipa Gordon in *Anne of the Island* as they prepared to leave Kingsport for the holidays:

> *I'm going home to an old country farmhouse, once green, rather faded now, set among leafless apple orchards. There is a brook below and a December fir wood beyond, where I've heard harps swept by the fingers of rain and wind. There'll be love there, Phil — faithful, tender love, such as I'll never find anywhere else in the world — love that's waiting for me.*

To re-create Anne's beloved Green Gables in gingerbread, you will need:

- *Gingerbread (recipe follows)*
- *Cookie sheets*
- *Parchment paper (optional)*
- *Brown paper (grocery bags are ideal)*
- *Pencil*
- *Ruler*
- *Scissors*
- *Rolling pin*
- *Extra flour*
- *Small sharp knife*
- *Pastry wheel (optional)*
- *Sturdy tray or breadboard, at least 9 by 14 inches (22.5 by 35 cm), for displaying the house*
- *Royal Icing (recipe follows)*
- *Pastry bag with decorating tips (optional) or several medium-sized zip-top plastic bags*
- *Green food colouring*
- *Cream-filled wafer cookies (about ½ by 3 inches/12 mm by 7.5 cm)*
- *Green sugar crystals*
- *Tiny red cinnamon candies*
- *1 yellow jellybean or candy gold dragee*
- *Cinnamon sticks or pretzel rods (optional)*

Base: 7 by 12 inches (18 by 30 cm)

Walls for large wing:
$6^1/2$ by $6^1/2$ inches (16 by 16 cm) (need 2)

Roof for large wing: $7^1/2$ by $5^1/4$ inches (19 by 13 cm) (need 2)

Drawn half-scale

Gable ends for large wing: *6 1/2 by 10 1/2 inches (16 by 26 cm) (need 2)*

Walls for small wing: 5 by 4 inches (13 by 10 cm) (need 2)

Chimney: 2 by 1 1/2 inches (5 by 3.8 cm), notched at one end to fit angle of roof (need 2)

Roof for small wing: 7 by 5 inches (18 by 13 cm) (need 2)

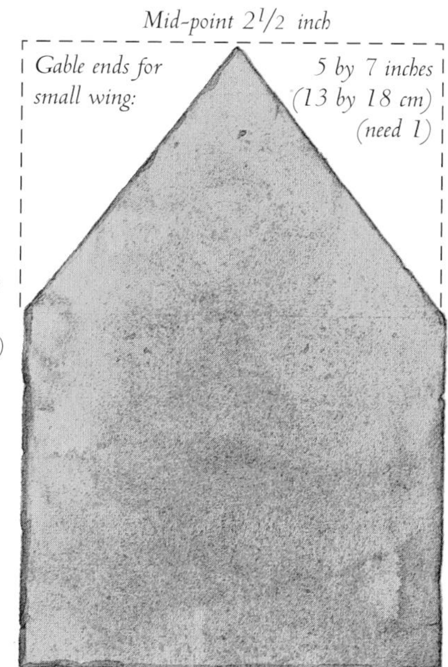

Gable ends for small wing: *5 by 7 inches (13 by 18 cm) (need 1)*

Baking the Gingerbread House

Make three recipes of the gingerbread. It is a stiff dough and is much easier to make in small batches than in one large batch. Chill the dough for about an hour before rolling it out.

½ cup	*butter, margarine or shortening*	125 mL
½ cup	*granulated sugar*	125 mL
¼ cup	*brown sugar*	50 mL
⅓ cup	*dark molasses*	75 mL
1	*egg*	1
2 tbsp	*water*	25 mL
3 cups	*all-purpose flour*	750 mL
1 tsp	*baking soda*	5 mL
1 tsp	*ground cinnamon*	5 mL
1½ tsp	*ground ginger*	7 mL
½ tsp	*salt*	2 mL

1 Cream the butter and sugars until the mixture is fluffy. Add the molasses, egg and water and mix thoroughly.

2 Mix the rest of the ingredients and add them ½ cup (125 mL) at a time to the butter mixture. More flour can be added, a ¼ cup (50 mL) at a time, if necessary, to make a stiff dough.

3 Wrap the dough in plastic wrap and chill it for an hour.

4 Make two more batches of gingerbread.

5 While the dough is chilling, make the patterns for the base, walls, roof and chimney sections of the house using the brown paper, pencil, ruler and scissors. Cut out the patterns from pages 34 and 35 and set them aside.

6 Preheat the oven to 350°F (180°C).

7 Spread a piece of parchment paper on the *back* of a cookie sheet (or lightly grease the cookie sheet if you prefer). With the rolling pin, roll a large piece of the gingerbread dough to ⅛-inch (3-mm) thickness directly on the cookie sheet. Patch in extra dough if necessary to make a rectangle 7 by 12 inches (18 by 30 cm). Lay the pattern for the base on top of the dough to check for size. Trim the edges with a sharp knife or pastry wheel, using the pattern and a ruler for a guide. This will be the base of the gingerbread

house. For ease in assembling the house later, make some shallow grooves in the base, about 1/4 inch (6 mm) from the edges, where the walls will go. Use the ruler to measure a groove 7 inches (18 cm) square for the main wing and a groove 5 inches (13 cm) square for the small wing (see diagram). The dull edge of a table knife, a chopstick or your little finger will do for pressing the groove into the dough.

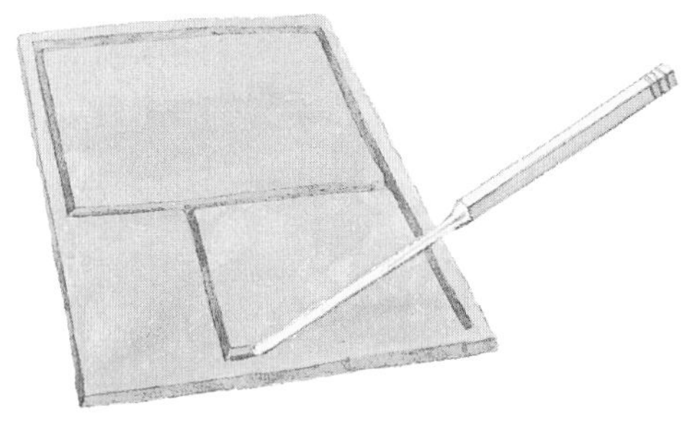

8 Bake the dough for ten minutes or until done.

9 Repeat the process to make the walls, gable ends, roof and chimney pieces (no grooves are necessary for these). Use a fresh piece of parchment paper with each baking. (Arrange as many pieces as you can on each baking sheet, so that it will take the least amount of baking time.)

10 Remove the pieces from the oven and let them rest for a few minutes on the cookie sheets, then carefully transfer them by sliding them, paper and all, onto flat racks or sheets of newspaper spread on a table. While the pieces are still warm, check them again for size and trim any rough edges if necessary. (Don't worry if the pieces are a tiny bit smaller than the measurements; the icing "glue" will fill in.) Any leftover gingerbread dough can be made into tree shapes to stand beside the finished house or cut into cookie shapes — stars, hearts, maple leaves, even lighthouses would be ideal for an Anne-related theme. Decorate the cookies with white or coloured icing, if you wish, and hang them on the tree or serve them as a Christmas treat.

Assembling the Gingerbread House

Once the pieces have cooled completely (wait several hours or even overnight for this), you can assemble them. This is much easier with two people than just one!

Make a recipe of Royal Icing:

3	*large egg whites*	*3*
½ tsp	*cream of tartar*	*2 mL*
pinch	*salt*	*pinch*
1 lb	*confectioner's sugar*	*500 g*

1 Beat the egg whites, cream of tartar and salt until foamy. Add the confectioner's sugar, beating until the mixture can hold a soft peak when the beaters are lifted out. Cover the mixture with a damp tea towel until you are ready to use it because it hardens quickly. Store any unused icing in an airtight container in the refrigerator.

2 Fill a pastry bag fitted with a large decorating tip about one-third full of Royal Icing. If you do not have a pastry bag, you can use a plastic squeeze bottle with a pointed tip (squeezable honey or mustard bottles are ideal) or even a zip-top plastic bag. Snip a tiny corner off the bottom of the zip-top bag for the icing to come through.

3 Set the gingerbread base piece on the display tray (you may want to line the tray with parchment paper, waxed paper or a paper doily). Put a few dots of Royal Icing on the bottom of the paper lining to hold it in place on the tray and a few dots of icing on the base to keep it from slipping.

4 Pipe a 7-inch (18-cm) line of icing on the base for the front gable piece and a 7-inch (18-cm) line for one side wall. Spread some icing on the bottoms and adjoining edges of the two pieces and set them into place, pressing them firmly together at the corners and making sure they are standing straight up. Repeat the process with the back gable piece and the remaining side wall. Assemble the small wing in the same way. Refill the icing bag as necessary.

5 When the walls are firmly in place, spread the top edges of the gables and side walls with icing and set the roof pieces on, beginning with the larger roof. Spread the centre seam of each roof piece with icing before joining it to the other piece. Spread one of the chimney pieces with icing and "glue" the other piece to it, like a sandwich. Set it in the centre of the large roof, attaching it with more icing.

Decorating the Gingerbread House

1 With the pastry bag now fitted with a small piping tip (or with the twist-top of the plastic bottle closed a bit for a smaller line of icing or a fresh zip-top bag with a smaller hole snipped out of the corner), decorate the roof with icing "shingles," the roof and chimney edges with "icicles," and pipe on window panes. Make two windows upstairs and two downstairs on the large wing and one window on the small wing. Make a "woodpile" with cinnamon sticks (or pretzel rods cut to 2-inch/ 5-cm lengths), held together with icing.

2 Mix about two cups (500 mL) of the white icing with drops of green food colouring until you have a nice, rich Green Gablesy green. With a sharp knife, cut the wafer cookies into ten pieces, about ⅜ inch (9 mm) wide and the length of your windows. These will be the shutters. Split the wafers open and scrape off the creamy insides. Spread one side and the edges of each of the wafers with green icing, put some icing on the backs of the wafers and "glue" them on either side of each of the windows. Cut two pieces of wafer cookies, ⅜ inch (9 mm) wide, to fit on either side of the door. Glue a whole wafer right across the top of the door, as well as the two side pieces, to give the effect of a porch. Spread green icing on the gables; sprinkle with green sugar, if desired.

3 Outline the front door with green icing. Make a wreath for the door and evergreen garlands for the porch and windowsills with short squiggles of green icing and decorate them with small red cinnamon candies. Cut off the top of a yellow jellybean (or use a gold dragee) and stick it on the door for a doorknob.

4 Continue decorating the house as you wish, perhaps with some green shrubbery, a trellis on the small wing, more windows and doors on the sides and the back of the house, etc.

5 Sift a bit of powdered sugar over the whole house to resemble freshly fallen snow. Set the completed gingerbread house on a table and enjoy it throughout the season.

Matthew's Sleigh-Bell Door Chimes

"The snow crisped under the runners; the music of the bells tinkled through the ranks of tall pointed firs, snow-laden." When the red dirt roads of Prince Edward Island were covered with a thick layer of snow, the buggy that Matthew drove to Bright River when he met Anne at the depot in June had to be stored in the barn until spring. The sorrel mare was hitched up instead to a sleigh for travelling in wintertime. Sleigh-bells were hung on the horse's harness so that they jingled merrily with every step.

To make a ribbon of jingle bells to remind you of Matthew's sleigh-bells at holiday time, you will need:

1 yard (1 metre) grosgrain ribbon, 2 inches (5 cm) wide

1 brass ring, 2-inch (5-cm) diameter

4 jingle bells, 1-inch (2.5-cm) diameter

1 tassel in a coordinating colour, 3 inches (7.5 cm) long

Matching thread

Needle

1 Slide the brass ring onto the ribbon until it is at the centre point. Fold the ribbon in half over the ring.

Pin the ribbon in place. Stitch the four jingle bells onto the double thickness of ribbon, spacing them about 4 inches (10 cm) apart. Fold the ends of the ribbon into a point and stitch the excess onto the back of the ribbon. Sew the tassel onto the point of the ribbon.

2 Hang the sleigh-bells on a small nail or hook on the back of the front door so they will jingle merrily whenever the door is opened or closed. (If you prefer, attach a bit of ribbon to the top of the brass ring and tie it on the doorknob.)

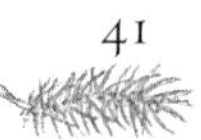

Gifts to Make for "Kindred Spirits"

"Why — why — Matthew, is that for me? Oh, Matthew!"

ANNE OF GREEN GABLES, XXV

The most famous Christmas gift in Anne's story was the puff-sleeved dress that Matthew asked Mrs. Rachel Lynde to make for Anne. It was a dream come true, for Anne had never had a pretty, fashionable dress before — Matthew had thought of the perfect gift for her.

Christmas gifts in Anne's day were usually handmade and were not always so elaborate — knitted lace, mittens and "wristers" (knitted cuffs that could be slipped on the wrists under sleeves to keep out draughts), warm mufflers, monogrammed handkerchiefs and stationery were often in the big Christmas basket or under the tree.

You can make gifts for your family and friends, too. Some of the following handmade items were mentioned as gifts in the Anne books, while others were inspired by the books and can be made as reminders of Green Gables.

A Green Gables Tea Cosy

Tea was served at Green Gables with every meal and anytime in between. The kettle was always ready on the old Waterloo wood stove in the kitchen for a fresh pot of tea, especially if company happened to come by. A tea cosy is handy for keeping the tea hot and here is one to remind you of Green Gables with each pot you brew.

You will need:

⅓ yard (30 cm) white quilted cotton fabric

30 inches (75 cm) dark green grosgrain ribbon, 1-inch (2.5-cm) wide

32 inches (80 cm) dark green grosgrain ribbon, ½-inch (12-mm) wide

White thread and dark green thread

Chalk or pencil for marking cloth

1 skein dark green embroidery floss

Embroidery needle

1 gold button, ¼-inch (6-mm) round

Pins

Scissors

Sewing machine or needle

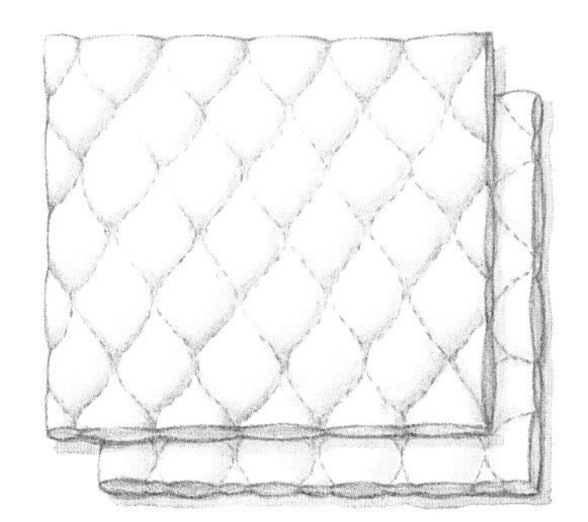

1 From the quilted fabric, cut two pieces 12 by 14 inches (30 by 35 cm). Fold each in half to measure 12 by 7 inches (30 by 18 cm). On the 12-inch (30-cm) side opposite the fold, mark 7 inches (18 cm) from the bottom. Cut from the mark up to the top of the centre fold on both pieces as shown. Unfold the pieces; select one for the front and place it right side up on a flat surface.

2 Cut the 1-inch (2.5-cm) wide green ribbon into four pieces: one 3-inch (7.5-cm) piece, one 4-inch (10-cm) piece, one 6-inch (15-cm) piece, and one 8-inch (20-cm) piece. Slightly overlapping the pieces, arrange them to form the green gable at the pointed top of the white fabric (ends of the ribbon will extend a little bit beyond the fabric). Pin the ribbon pieces in place and stitch around the edges to the fabric; trim ends even with fabric base.

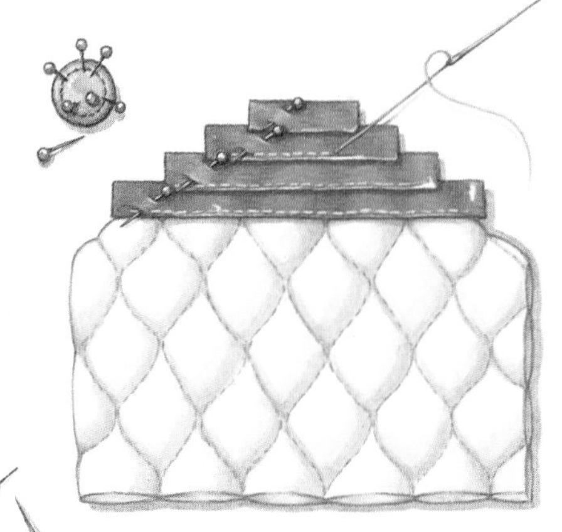

3 Cut the ½-inch (12-mm) wide green ribbon into pieces for window shutters and door: two 3-inch (7.5-cm) pieces, four 2 ¼-inch (5.5-cm) pieces, four 2-inch (5-cm) pieces and three 2 ¾-inch (7-cm) pieces. With tailor's chalk (or pencil) sketch in the windows and door as shown.

4 Pin the two 3-inch (7.5-cm) pieces of ribbon on for the door frame. Pin the three 2 ¾-inch (7-cm) pieces, slightly overlapping them as you did for the large gable, and stitch together. Fold and cut from the top centre to the bottom corner to form a triangular piece. Turn sides under about ⅛ inch (3 mm) and press. Place at the top of the door frame pieces and adjust for fit. Pin in place.

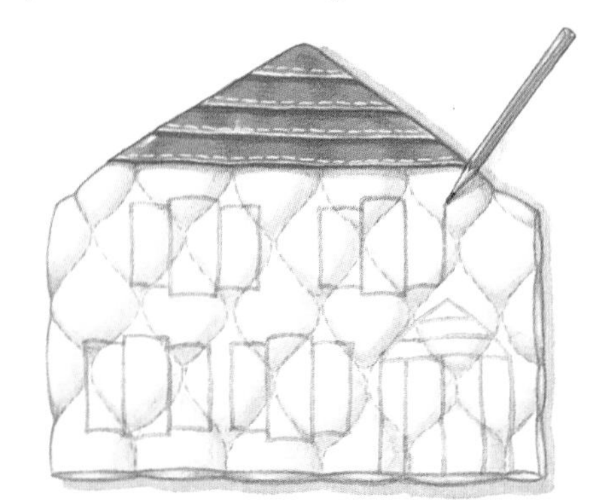

5 Turn ends of remaining ribbon pieces under ⅛ inch (3 mm) and press. Lay four 2 ¼-inch (5.5-cm) pieces of ribbon in place for the window shutters beside the front door; lay four 2-inch (5-cm) pieces in place for the upstairs window shutters. Pin. Stitch door and shutter pieces in place.

6 With two strands of embroidery floss, outline-stitch the window frames and door panels (see illustration).

7 Sew a tiny gold button on the door for the doorknob.

8 Pin the two pieces of quilted fabric with right sides together. Stitch together the walls and the roof with a ½-inch (12-mm) seam allowance. Turn up the bottom edge and hem.

9 You might want to embroider a tiny candle in Anne's window above the door as a reminder of Anne and Diana's secret signalling system.

Other options are little strips of lace in the windows for curtains and a dark red ribbon loop on the roof peak for a chimney.

Christmas Ribbon Cushion

Cushions and pillows covered in needlepoint, crewel embroidery, tapestry, lace and other rich fabrics were important decorative accessories in Victorian homes. They were usually stuffed with feathers, cotton batting or cloth scraps but occasionally pine needles or soft fir needles were used instead. Anne and Diana made such cushions for themselves — Anne liked to use hers for her naps in hopes that she would dream of being a wood-nymph! Perhaps you would like to make a Christmas Ribbon Cushion for a friend and one for yourself as well. You can make it in traditional red and green colours or in softer pinks, greens and white to coordinate with your Wild-Rose Christmas theme.

For each cushion, you will need:

- *1/3 yard (30 cm) green cotton velvet fabric*
- *2 yards (2 metres) striped ribbon, 1 3/8-inch (34-mm) wide*
- *2 yards (2 metres) plaid or floral ribbon, 1 3/8-inch (34-mm) wide*
- *Scissors*
- *Matching thread*
- *Polyester fibre-fill pillow stuffing (5 to 8 ounces/150 to 250g) or pine needles if you prefer!*
- *Needle and pins*

1 Cut the velvet into two 12-inch (30-cm) squares. One will be the top of the cushion, the other will be the back. Set one piece aside while you make the top.

2 Cut the ribbon into 12-inch (30-cm) lengths. Lay six pieces of one colour ribbon vertically on top of the velvet, placing the first piece ½ inch (12 mm) from the edge of the velvet. Leave about ½ inch (12 mm) between each piece of ribbon, and adjust the spacing so that the pieces are evenly placed. Make sure that ½ inch (12 mm) of velvet is showing on the right-hand side and left-hand side for a seam allowance. Pin the ends of each ribbon to the velvet.

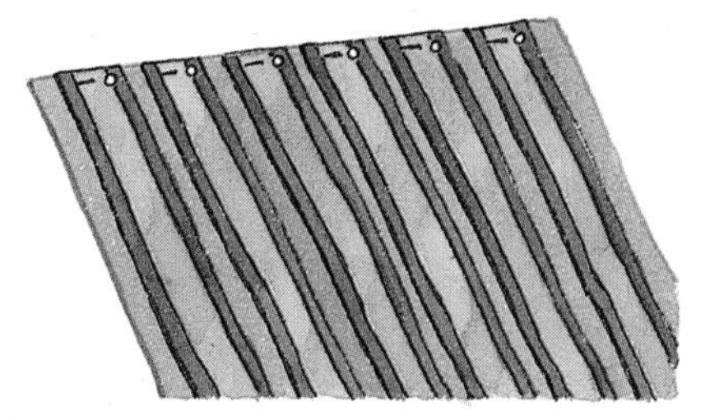

3 Weave the other colour ribbon, cut in 12-inch (30-cm) lengths, in and out of the ribbon that is pinned to the velvet. Leave about ½ inch (12 mm) between each piece of ribbon. Adjust the ribbons as before, leaving ½ inch (12 mm) on the top and bottom for a seam allowance.

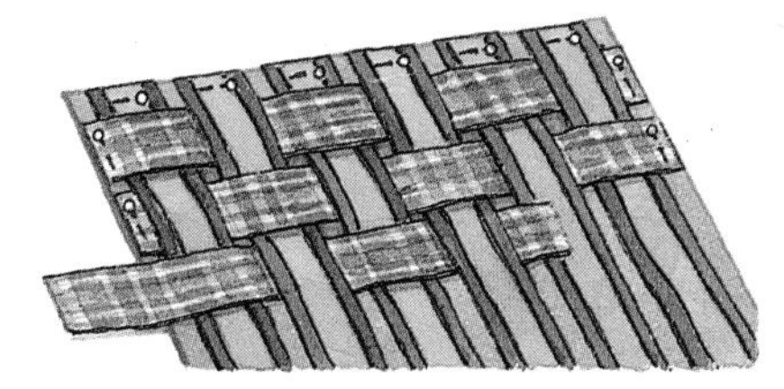

4 Stitch the ends of the ribbons to the velvet about ⅜ inch (9 mm) from the edges of the fabric.

5 Place the ribbon-covered velvet right side up on a flat surface and place the other square of velvet on top of it, right side down. Stitch around all sides of the cushion about ½ inch (12 mm) from the edges, leaving an opening of about 4 inches (10 cm) on one side for turning the cushion inside out. Clip the corners and turn the cushion inside out. Press the edges if necessary.

6 Stuff the cushion until it is as plump as you like. Stitch the opening of the cushion closed.

Anne's Beaded Slippers

After Anne had received Matthew's puff-sleeved dress, Diana ran over with another unexpected gift, this one from Miss Josephine Barry, Diana's aunt from Charlottetown.

Anne opened the box and peeped in. First a card with "For the Anne-girl and Merry Christmas," written on it; and then, a pair of the daintiest little kid slippers, with beaded toes and satin bows and glistening buckles.

The slippers were just right to wear with her new dress to the concert that evening. Otherwise, she would have had to borrow Ruby Gillis's slippers so that she would be properly attired for her part as the fairy queen.

To make a version of Anne's beaded slippers for a very special gift, you will need:

---

1 pair ballet-style slippers (made of velvet or finely knitted satin)

Tiny (1/8-inch/3-mm) pearl beads (available in fabric stores or bridal shops)

Needle

Thread to match slippers or pearls

Scissors

Small ribbon rose or satin bow (optional)

---

1 Stitch the pearl beads on the toes of the slippers in a design of your choice. The design can be very simple, as shown here, or more elaborate, depending on your skill with the needle and your patience.

2 You can add satin bows or ribbon roses (or both) to each toe of the slippers, if you wish. If the slippers already have little satin bows on the toes, you can stitch a small ribbon rose on each. These are slippers any fairy queen or wood-nymph or dryad would be delighted to wear!

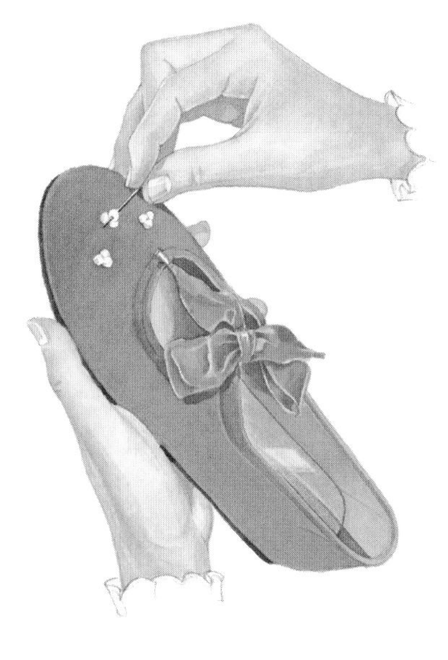

Matthew's Fringed Tartan Muffler

Matthew spent many cold winter hours in the Green Gables barn, tending to the horse and cows. He also chopped great quantities of wood for the Waterloo woodstove in the kitchen as well as for the wood-stoves in the parlour and dining-sitting room throughout the winter. Then there were those times when he had to drive the sleigh, taking the brunt of the cold breezes while Anne and Marilla, wrapped in warm robes, sat more cozily in the sheltered seat.

Anne may well have made a warm, woollen muffler for Matthew to wear during the winter. A cheerful tartan plaid would have been the perfect choice, since Matthew and Marilla's parents had come to Prince Edward Island years before from Scotland.

To make a tartan muffler for the Matthew in your life, you will need:

1/3 yard (30 cm) soft woven wool in the plaid of your choice, 60 inches (150 cm) wide

---

Scissors

Thread (optional)

Needle (optional)

---

1 Trim the long edges of the fabric as evenly as possible. Fringe the long edges to about 1/4 inch (6 mm) by gently pulling one long thread at a time out of the fabric. Fringe the short ends to about 1/2 inch (12 mm) by pulling one short thread at a time out of the fabric.

2 If you wish, take a few stitches in each corner of the scarf to make sure the threads do not unravel further. You can also use a drop of clear glue, nail polish or commercial fray-stopping solution.

Marilla's Black Lace Shawl

Early in Anne's new life at Green Gables, a crisis occurred. Marilla's heirloom amethyst brooch was missing and Marilla was sure that Anne had taken it. Anne insisted that she had not, but Marilla wouldn't listen. She forbade Anne's attending the Sunday School picnic until she "confessed." Anne, desperate to go to the picnic and have her first taste of ice cream, finally did confess, only to have Marilla refuse permission again, as "punishment." Not until it was nearly time for the picnic to begin did Marilla happen to find the amethyst brooch. It had become caught in her best black lace shawl. She apologized to Anne and helped her get ready to go to the picnic after all. Since Marilla's shawl had been torn by the amethyst brooch, perhaps Anne gave her a new one at Christmas.

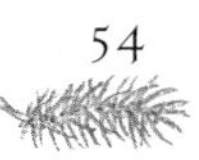

To make a black lace shawl for the Marilla in your life, you will need:

---

1 yard (1 metre) black lace, 60 inches (150 cm) wide

3 ½ yards (3 ½ metres) black lace edging, ½ inch (12 mm) wide

Scissors

Needle and pins

Black thread

1 The lace fabric should be finished on the long edges when you buy it.

2 Cut the lace edging into two equal lengths. Pin it to each of the two unfinished ends of the lace fabric.

3 Stitch in place, turning under the raw ends at each edge.

Other gifts to make for "kindred spirits" might include Diana's Sweetheart Collar (page 66), Anne's Braided Velvet Headband (page 65), Anne's Velvet Muff (page 62) or a Necklace of Roseberries (page 17). *The Anne of Green Gables Treasury* contains instructions for potpourri, sachets, pressed-flower pictures and bookmarks, crocheted lace edging and many other items that Anne and her friends enjoyed.

Wild-Rose Gift Package

Continue the Wild-Rose Christmas theme when wrapping your gifts, especially those for "kindred spirits." Decorate larger packages with handmade Tissue Roses (see page 6) or sprigs of fresh evergreen. For smaller packages, this luxurious wild-rose wrapping technique looks much too pretty to unwrap!

For a 3-inch (7.5-cm) square gift box, you will need:

15-inch (38-cm) square white net or other sheer fabric

15-inch (38-cm) square of pink gift-wrap tissue or fabric

Scissors

½ yard (45 cm) green ribbon, ⅛ inch (3 mm) wide

Rose-Leaf Gift Tag (see page 57)

1 Spread the net on a flat surface and lay the pink tissue or fabric on top of the net. Trim the net and tissue into a circle 15 inches (38 cm) in diameter. Set the gift box in the centre, gather the net and tissue at the top of the gift and tie firmly with the narrow green ribbon. Fluff the net and tissue to resemble a rose.

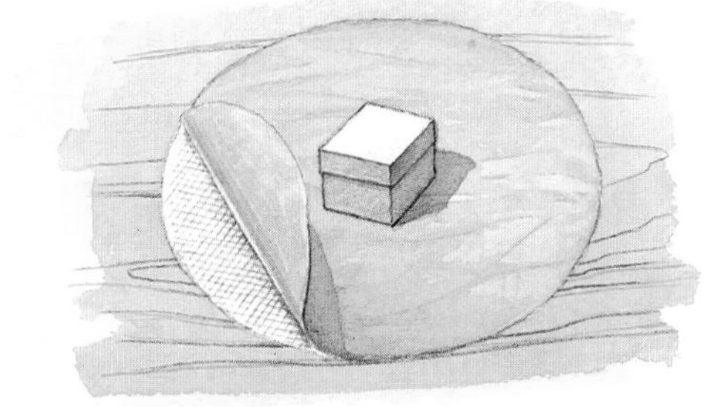

2 If you like, decorate the gift package with a tissue rose (see page 6). Attach a rose-leaf gift tag (see page 57).

3 For an unforgettable touch, put a drop of rose-scented cologne on your finger and rub it gently in several places on the net.

Rose-Leaf Gift Tag

Cut a rose-leaf shape from green paper to make a tag to accompany your Wild-Rose Gift Package. You can also tape a few of these to the stems of your Tissue Roses, if you wish.

Green construction paper or green index card, 3 by 5 inches (7.5 by 13 cm)

Pencil

Scissors

Green pen

Glue (optional)

Green glitter (optional)

1 Following the pattern below, sketch a rose-leaf pattern on the construction paper. The leaf should measure about 2 by 3 inches (5 by 7.5 cm). Cut out the leaf.

To:
From:

2 With green ink, outline the edge of the leaf. If you like, put a thread of glue along the edge and sprinkle green glitter on the glue. Allow ink and/or glue to dry.

3 With green ink, write a "to-from" message with the recipient's name and your own on the leaf.

4 Punch a small hole in the stem end of the leaf (start the hole with a pin prick and enlarge it slightly with a pencil point). Put one end of the ribbon already tied to the wild-rose gift package through the hole, slide the gift tag up close to the rose and tie the ribbon in a bow to hold the tag securely to the package.

Holiday Finery

Christmas was only a fortnight off. A nice new dress would be the very thing for a present.

ANNE OF GREEN GABLES, XXV

Once Matthew figured out that Anne "was not dressed like the other girls," he decided to give her a new dress for Christmas, one with her much-wished-for puffed sleeves. On Christmas evening, Anne proudly wore the first fashionable dress she had ever owned.

When the ladies of Anne's time dressed up for special occasions, there were many accessories added to their fine clothes, such as delicate filigree jewellery, fancy combs and hair clips, fans, silver nosegay holders, lace collars and scarves, and elaborate hats.

Girls dressed more simply than adults, but their dresses were made in much the same styles as the grown-up versions. Skirts were full and were worn at mid-calf or slightly longer; girls did not wear long skirts until they were at least seventeen. They also wore their long hair loose, held back from the face with ribbons or plaited in braids. When they began to wear long skirts, they pinned their hair up neatly.

Here are some suggestions for holiday fashions that you can wear today, inspired by those of Anne's era.

Diana's Christmas Skirt with Ribbon Sash

Diana had pretty clothes and plenty of them. Until Matthew gave Anne her puff-sleeved dress after she had been at Green Gables nearly two years, Anne could only imagine that her own plain dresses had "lovely lace frills and three-puffed sleeves."

Christmas is the time for festive, colourful party clothes and this simple-to-make skirt will be just right for any special party or concert.

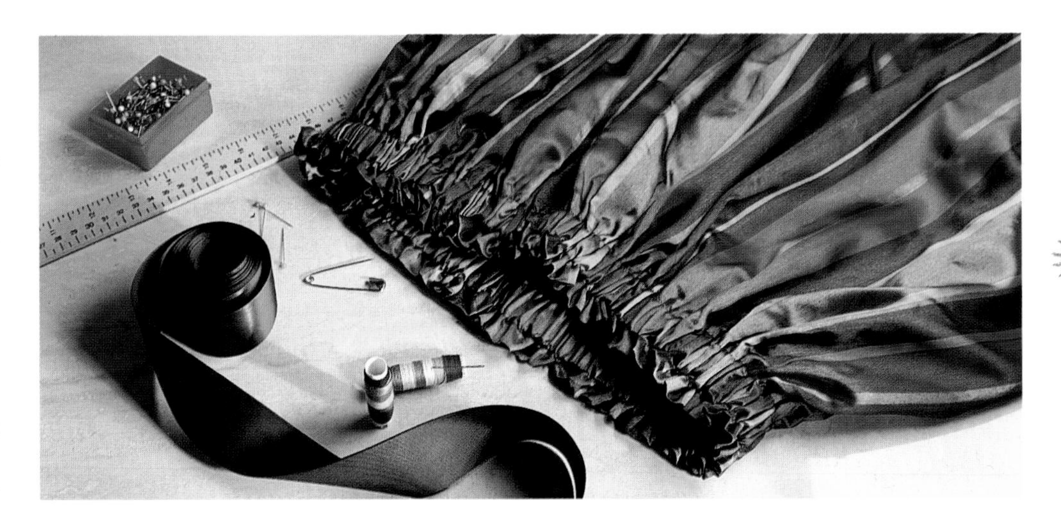

- 2 yards (2 metres) taffeta or silk-like fabric, 45 inches (115 cm) wide
- Matching thread
- Needle and pins
- Scissors
- 24 inches (60 cm) elastic, 1 inch (2.5 cm) wide
- Large safety pin
- 4 yards (4 metres) coordinating satin ribbon, 1 ½ inches (38 mm) wide

1 Cut the fabric into two equal lengths.

2 With right sides together, stitch up the two long sides of the fabric. Press the seams open with a warm iron.

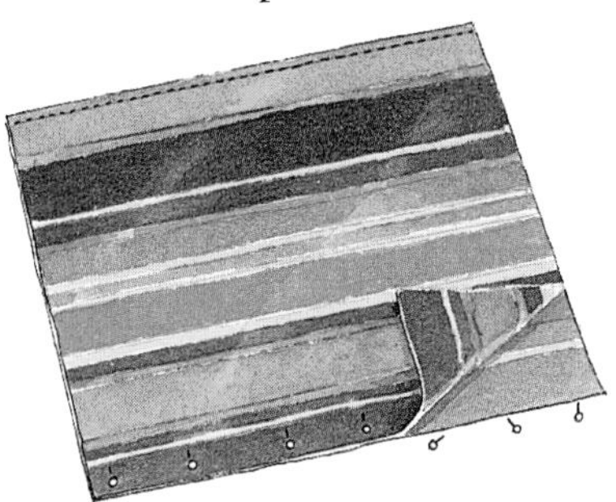

3 Turn down 1/4 inch (6 mm) of the top edge of the "tube" toward the inside and press. Then turn down 2 inches (5 cm) more and press.

4 Make a line of stitching about 1/2 inch (12 mm) down from the top edge of the fold. Stitch a second line about 1 1/8 inches (3 cm) down from the top stitching line, but leave an opening of about 3 inches (7.5 cm).

5 You should now have a "tunnel" along the top edge of the skirt for the elastic to go through. Attach a large safety pin to one end of the elastic and thread the elastic through the tunnel, using the safety pin to push it along.

6 Adjust the elastic to fit the size of your waist and sew the two ends of the elastic together. Sew up the opening in the waistband.

7 Check the skirt for length. The skirt should come just about to your mid-calf when it is finished. Allow three extra inches for a hem; trim off extra length.

8 Turn up 1/4 inch (6 mm) of the skirt toward the inside and press. Turn up 2 3/4 to 3 inches (7 to 7.5 cm) more for a hem and press. Pin up the hem and stitch by hand.

9 Wear the skirt with a ribbon sash tied over the gathered waistband. Tie the sash in a full bow with the ends in long streamers.

10 A pretty blouse, perhaps with "lovely puffed sleeves" like Anne's Christmas dress from Matthew, would be a perfect finishing touch!

Anne's Velvet Muff

A muff was a very popular winter accessory. It was almost like a little pillow wrapped around the hands to keep them warm while the girls went riding in a sleigh or walking in the cold night air. Sometimes muffs were made of fur, but they were also made of fine fabrics as well. Once Marilla saw how much fashionable clothes meant to Anne, it is likely that she added a muff to her wardrobe.

A black velvet muff is ideal for the holiday season; line the inside with a contrasting colour for an elegant touch.

13- by 20-inch (32- by 50-cm) piece of black cotton velvet or velveteen

11- by 18-inch (28- by 45-cm) piece of contrasting velvet for the lining

11- by 18- by 1-inch (28- by 45- by 2.5-cm) piece of cotton batting

1/3 yard (20 cm) white net

Needle and pins

Black thread

1 1/2 yards (1 1/2 metres) black velvet cording or ribbon

1 Place the piece of black velvet, right side up, on a flat surface. Lay the contrasting piece of velvet lining

on top of it, right side down, with one long edge of the lining lying exactly along one long edge of the black velvet. There should be 1 inch (2.5 cm) of the black velvet showing along each side and 2 inches (5 cm) showing along the other long edge.

2 Pin the two pieces together and stitch along the side where the two fabrics are even, making a 1/2-inch (12-mm) seam. Remove the pins.

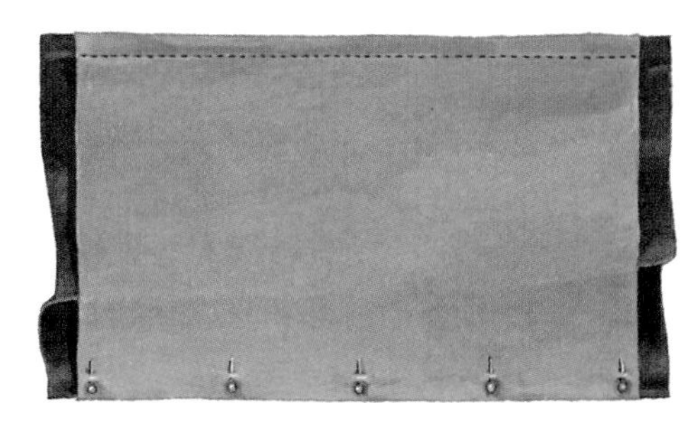

3 Now match the other long edges of the two fabrics. The black fabric is wider than your lining, but don't worry about that; just match the edges and pin them. Stitch together with a 1/2-inch (12-mm) seam. Remove the pins.

4 Turn the velvet inside out. There will be 1 inch (2.5 cm) of black velvet showing on the open ends of the lining and ½ inch (12 mm) along the stitched sides.

5 Wrap a piece of net lightly around the batting just so that it holds the batting in place. Baste the net closed. Slip the "package" of netted batting into the velvet "tube," leaving the inch of black velvet showing at each end.

6 Fold the black velvet over toward the contrasting velvet at each end, pinning the openings closed. Hand-stitch the ends closed and remove the pins. Fold the muff in half, pin the two ends together, and hand-stitch. You now should have a cozy tube of velvet.

7 The seam should be at the bottom of the muff. Knot each end of the ribbon or cording. Stitch one end to the top of one side of the muff, just near the lining; sew the other end to the other side of the muff. To wear the muff, hang it around your neck and slip your hands into each end.

Anne's Braided Velvet Headband

When Anne impulsively tried to dye her hair "a beautiful raven black," it turned a ghastly shade of green instead. There was nothing to do but cut it all off! In a few weeks, however, her hair began to grow out into short, silky auburn curls that "were held in place by a very jaunty black velvet ribbon and bow."

Make your own black velvet headband for the holidays or any festive occasion. It will be particularly charming worn along with the velvet muff.

For one headband, you will need:

2 yards (2 metres) black velvet cord

24 inches (60 cm) black velvet ribbon

Scissors

Black thread

Needle

1 Cut the cord into three pieces, each 24 inches (60 cm) long. Stitch the three pieces together at one end and braid them all the way to the other end. Check to see if the braid will fit across the top of your head, from just under one ear to just under the other ear. Trim the ends if necessary and stitch them firmly together.

2 Cut the ribbon into two equal pieces. Sew the end of one piece to one end of the braid and repeat with the other piece of ribbon on the other end of the braid.

3 To wear the headband, place it across the top of your head and tie the ends of the ribbon in a bow under your hair at the back of your head.

Diana's Sweetheart Collar

White collars and cuffs were often made separately from blouses and shirts so that they could be washed more easily. A romantic little heart-shaped sweetheart collar would have suited Diana very nicely.

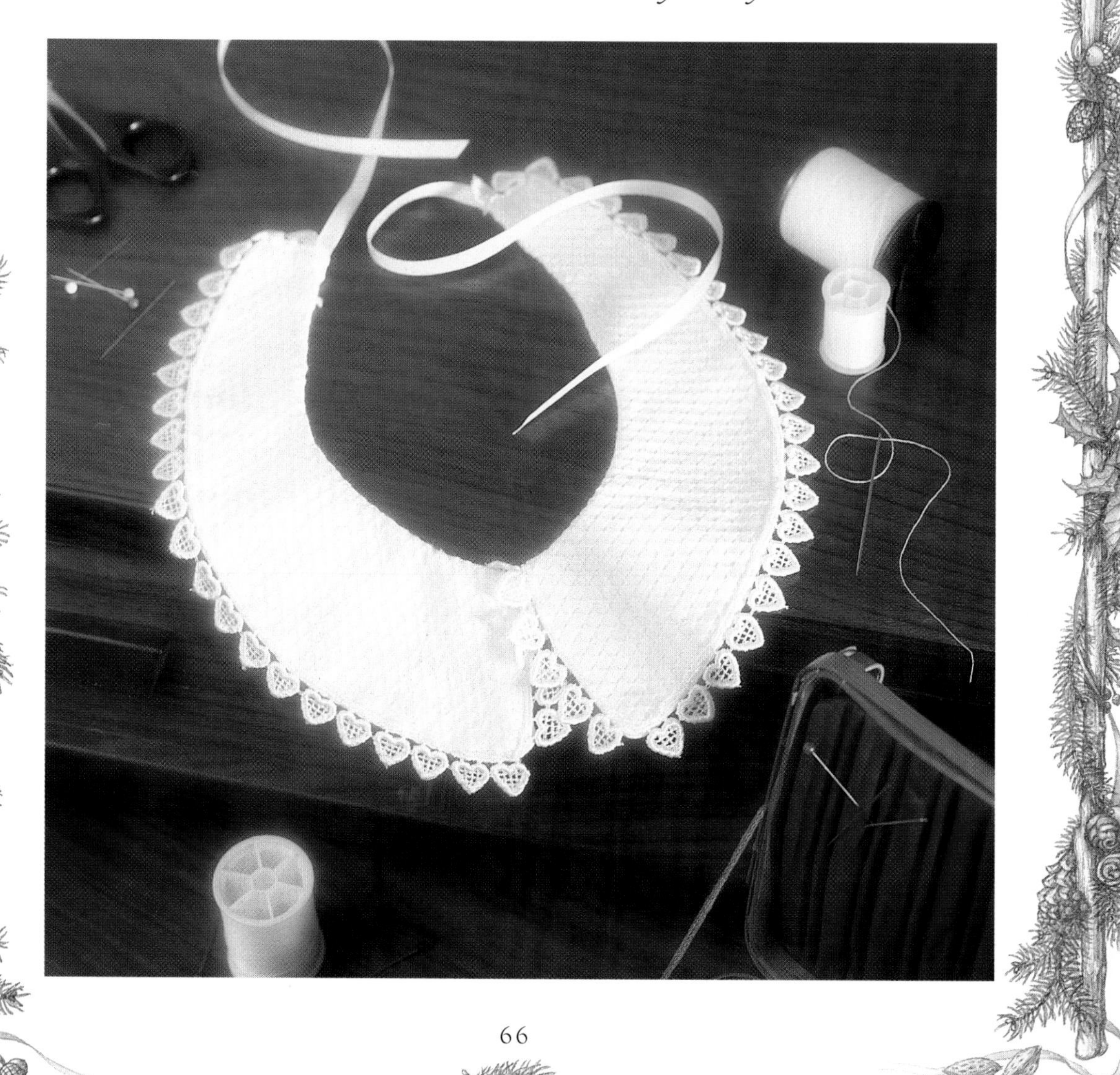

To make one sweetheart collar, you will need:

Tissue paper

1/3 yard (30 cm) white cotton piqué fabric

1 yard (1 metre) narrow lace edging

White thread

Needle and pins

24 inches (60 cm) narrow white satin ribbon

Scissors

---

1 Trace the pattern below onto tissue paper, enlarging it to fit nicely around your neck. (You may also trace around the collar of one of your own blouses for a pattern, if you prefer.)

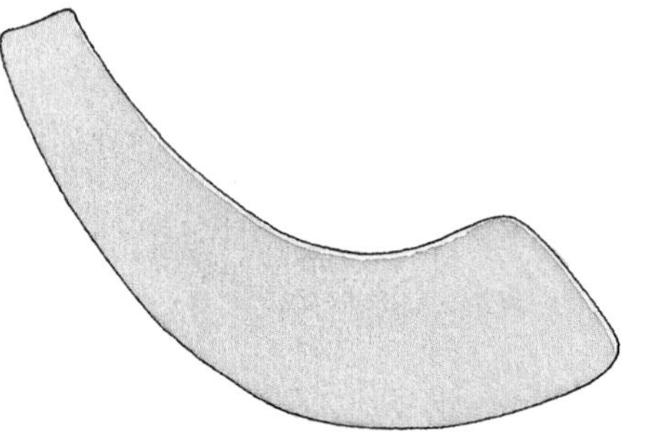

2 Fold the fabric in two and place the pattern on the fabric. Allowing 1/2 inch (12 mm) all around for a seam allowance, cut out two pieces. Move the pattern and cut out two more pieces.

3 Pin two collar pieces together with the right sides of the fabric facing each other. Stitch the pieces together with a 1/2-inch (12-mm) seam, leaving a 2-inch (5-cm) opening on the inside edge. With a warm iron, press the pieces flat. Trim the seam allowance to 1/4 inch (6 mm). Turn the pieces inside out; press. Stitch the opening closed.

4 Repeat with the remaining two collar pieces. Stitch the finished two pieces together where they meet at the front.

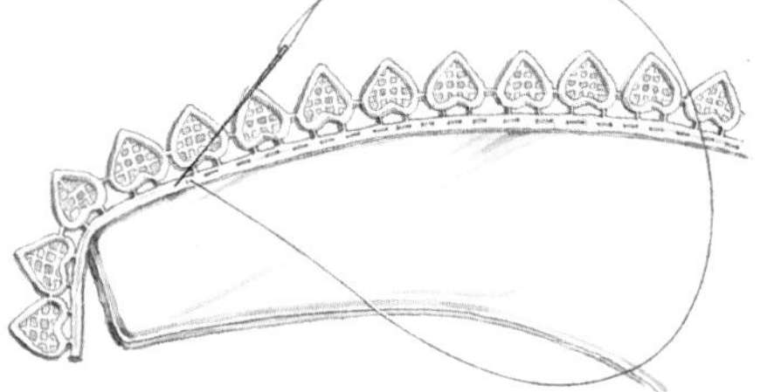

5 Hand-stitch, with tiny stitches, the lace edging around the outside edge of the collar pieces as shown. Stitch two lengths of narrow ribbon where the collar pieces meet at the back. Place the collar around your neck and tie the ribbon in a bow at the back of your neck.

Avonlea Christmas Concert
Avonlea Town Hall
December 25
Choruses Recitations
Dialogues Tableaux
Refreshments
WELCOME

Holiday Fun

All the Avonlea scholars were in a fever of excitement that day, for the hall had to be decorated and a last grand rehearsal held. The concert came off in the evening and was a pronounced success. The little hall was crowded; all the performers did excellently well, but Anne was the bright particular star of the occasion. . . .

ANNE OF GREEN GABLES, XXV

One favourite Christmas custom in Avonlea was the Christmas Concert. The first of these concerts that Anne was a part of was held on Christmas night at the Avonlea Hall. The schoolteacher, Anne's beloved Miss Stacy, proposed that her scholars "should get up a concert ... for the laudable purpose of helping to pay for a schoolhouse flag." Anne "threw herself into the undertaking heart and soul." The program included six choruses, several "dialogues," recitations and a tableau. The hall was decorated especially for the occasion, too.

Why not have a Christmas Concert of your own, as Anne and her friends did? Here are some suggestions.

An Avonlea Christmas Concert

Selecting the Performers

Several weeks ahead of time, invite six or eight friends to participate in the concert. Choose a time, date and place for the concert—the family room of your house, for instance.

Inviting the Guests

Make up a guest list (parents, brothers and sisters, and friends of the performers) and design your invitations. Send them to all on your list.

Invitation Card

Here is an idea for an invitation card that echoes the Wild-Rose Christmas theme.

For each invitation, you will need:

1 paper lace doily, 9 inches (23 cm) square

1 light green index card or other lightweight pastel green card stock, 5 by 7 inches (13 by 18 cm)

Coloured pens (especially green, brown, pink)

Glue

24 inches (60 cm) pink ribbon, 1/8 inch (3 mm) wide

Scissors

1 Fold the corners of the doily to meet at the centre; crease the edges. Open the doily and place it on a flat surface.

2 Cut the bottom 2 inches (5 cm) off the index card so that you have a 5-inch (13-cm) square. Write the invitation on the card. Decorate the card as you wish — we sketched one of the Avonlea "mottoes" made up of twigs at the bottom of our invitation. Glue the card to the centre of the doily.

3 Cut the ribbon into two pieces. Thread one through two facing corners of the doily; thread the second piece through the two remaining corners. Tie the corners over the written invitation as shown.

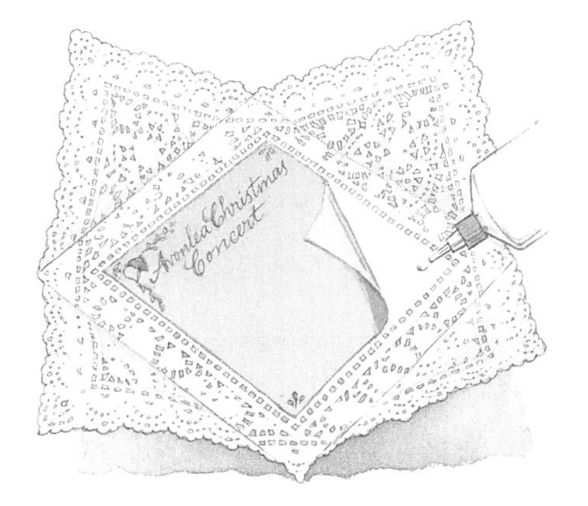

4 Hand-deliver the invitations or slip them into large white envelopes to mail.

PLANNING THE PROGRAM

Let each friend choose a poem to recite, a song to sing, a scene from a play to act out, or a piece to play on a musical instrument. Maybe several friends will want to perform something together. Plan for the concert to last no more than an hour.

Here are some suggestions for a Christmas concert, Avonlea-style:

The Processional

> *"We are all to march in two by two after the audience is seated, while Emma White plays a march on the organ."*
>
> ANNE OF GREEN GABLES, XXIV

After the audience is seated, you are ready to begin your concert. The processional music can be played on an instrument or sung by the performers as they come down the aisle. Choose any song you like; two popular Christmas processional songs are "O Come, All Ye Faithful" and "Once in Royal David's City." The performers can "march in two by two," lining up on the stage for the first act.

Christmas Carols

> *"We're going to have six choruses and Diana is to sing a solo."*
>
> ANNE OF GREEN GABLES, XXIV

To start the concert, the whole group of performers (and the audience, too, perhaps) can sing a few familiar holiday songs. Most of the ones we know today were also popular in Anne's day — "Deck the Halls," "God Rest Ye Merry, Gentlemen," "Joy to the World," and so many more. One Christmas carol that would evoke the image of Prince Edward Island nicely for your concert is "I Saw Three Ships."

Poems and Readings

> *"I'm in two dialogues — 'The Society for the Suppression of Gossip' and 'The Fairy Queen.' The boys are going to have a dialogue, too. And I'm to have two recitations, Marilla. I just tremble when I think of it, but it's a nice thrilly kind of tremble."*
>
> ANNE OF GREEN GABLES, XXIV

"Dialogues" were little plays or skits that the Avonlea students performed and "recitations" were poems or literary passages that the students memorized and recited, usually as a "solo."

For your concert, let the performers select a holiday story to enact, such as Hans Christian Andersen's *The Little Match Girl* or a scene from Charles Dickens's *A Christmas Carol.* You might even want to enact a scene from *Anne of Green Gables* such as Anne's arrival at Green Gables (chapter III) or Anne's first encounter with Mrs. Rachel Lynde (chapter IX). Costumes and scenery can be as simple or as elaborate as you wish.

Some performers may want to recite and there are many holiday poems to choose from. Here are two short ones that would have been familiar to Anne's class:

In the Bleak Midwinter

by Christina Rossetti (1830–1894)

In the bleak midwinter,
Frosty wind made moan,
Earth stood hard as iron,
Water like a stone;
Snow had fallen, snow on snow,
Snow on snow,
In the bleak midwinter,
Long ago.

Our God, heaven cannot hold him,
Nor earth sustain;
Heaven and earth shall flee away
When he comes to reign;
In the bleak midwinter
A stable place sufficed
The Lord God almighty,
Jesus Christ.

Angels and archangels
May have gathered there,
Cherubim and seraphim
Thronged the air;
But his mother only,
In her maiden bliss,
Worshipped the beloved
With a kiss.

What can I give him,
Poor as I am?
If I were a shepherd,
I would bring a lamb;
If I were a wise man,
I would do my part;
Yet what I can give him —
Give my heart.

CHRISTMAS IS A-COMING
by "Mother Goose"

Christmas is a-coming,
The goose is getting fat.
Please put a penny
In the old man's hat.

If you haven't got a penny,
A ha'penny will do;
If you haven't got a ha'penny,
God bless you!

Someone may also want to recite or read the Christmas story from the Bible (Luke 2:1–14).

While the poems and recitations are going on, the tableau can be set up behind a curtain.

Tableau

"And we're to have a tableau at the last — 'Faith, Hope and Charity.' Diana and Ruby and I are to be in it, all draped in white with flowing hair. I'm to be Hope, with my hands clasped — so — and my eyes uplifted."

ANNE OF GREEN GABLES, XXIV

Tableaux were very popular in Anne's day and no concert would have been complete without one. They consisted of scenery and costumes to interpret a familiar concept, such as "Faith, Hope and Charity," or even a famous painting such as Gainsborough's "The Blue Boy" or da Vinci's "The Last Supper."

A curtain would be drawn across the stage while the tableau was set up and the actors took their places. Then the curtain was opened to reveal the tableau. The actors remained perfectly still for twenty or thirty seconds, and the curtain was drawn back across the stage.

If you would like to present a tableau at your concert, select a scene that will suit the number of performers and the occasion. Perhaps you would like to portray Mary and Joseph and the Baby Jesus in the stable with angels, shepherds and wise men in attendance. You could also choose a less serious scene, such as something from Clement Moore's poem "The Night Before Christmas" or even a scene from *Anne of Green Gables* — Matthew giving Anne the puff-sleeved dress (chapter XXV) or Anne and her friends portraying Elaine, the lily maid, (chapter XXVIII) from Tennyson's poem "The Idylls of the King."

Carols by Candlelight

End the concert with a few more carols and holiday songs. A very effective and moving way to do this is to give everyone — performers and audience members — a small candle (about 6 inches/15 cm long) that can be lit during the first carol while the lights in the room are dimmed. Ushers or performers can light a few candles and then light the first candle of each row of the audience; each audience member lights his or her candle from the candle of the person sitting next to him or her and, one by one, each candle in the room is lit. Provide cardboard holders (see page 79 for how to make Wild-Rose Bobèches) to keep the candle wax from dripping on hands. Carols to sing by candlelight might include "Away in a Manger" and "Silent Night." Blow out the candles, turn the lights up, and end the concert with "We Wish You a Merry Christmas."

Be sure to rehearse the concert enough so that everyone is familiar with his or her part and where it fits in the program schedule. Have one person make a list of all the necessary "props" and things that need to be done for the concert (turning lights on and off in the right places, for instance, or playing recorded music at certain times).

You might want to print up a special program listing the performers and their selections, the date and place of the concert, and any other information the audience would like to know. These can be passed out to each member of the audience as they enter the room. Or you can appoint an announcer to tell the audience what is next in the program and who will be performing.

Decorations

Anne's concert hall was decorated with "creeping spruce and fir mottoes with pink tissue paper roses in them." Perhaps the mottoes were the same ones L. M. Montgomery wrote of in her journal on December 19, 1891: "Welcome" and "We Delight In Our School" were spelled out with bits of fir and were put up on the walls of the town hall; pink and white tissue roses decorated the mottoes. Fir branches were arched over pictures and banners.

You can lay branches of evergreen on windowsills and across a mantel, nestling tissue roses (see page 6) in the greenery. Tie bits of evergreen around tissue roses with ribbon for nosegays that can be fastened to the ends of each row of chairs or carried by each program participant.

A simple but effective way to make a "motto" is to make letters out of twigs (each about 8 to 10 inches/20 to 25 cm long), gluing or wiring the twigs together to form the letters. Glue or wire small bits of evergreen onto the twig letters and wire the letters together to form the motto word or words. Glue or wire on tissue roses, if you wish. Twist a bit of wire to the back of the motto to make a loop and hang the motto over the doorway or above the stage area so that the guests will be sure to see it.

Refreshments

After the concert, invite your guests to the refreshment table. Serve something cold to drink and some cookies. Don't forget cups and napkins! Bouquets of tissue roses and evergreen would make beautiful table decorations.

Raspberry Cordial Punch

This Christmasy punch will remind you of Anne and Diana's ill-fated tea party when Anne thought she was serving Diana raspberry cordial but mistakenly poured Marilla's currant wine instead!

For one gallon (4.5 L) of punch (about 30 servings), you will need:

½ gal	*raspberry-cranberry juice, chilled*	*2.5 L*
1	*2-quart (2-L) bottle ginger ale, chilled*	*1*
	Ice ring or ice cubes	

1 Just before serving, combine the juice and ginger ale in a large punchbowl.

2 Add the ice ring or ice cubes. Serve immediately.

Ice Ring

1 Place a few raspberries, cranberries and mint leaves in each section of an ice-cube tray. Fill the sections with water and place the tray in the freezer to form ice cubes.

2 Select a ring mould that will fit the opening of your punch bowl. Fill the ring one-third full with cold water and set on a level rack in the freezer. When this layer has frozen, place the fruit-filled ice cubes on top and fill the rest of the mould with cold water. Put the mould back in the freezer until the water is frozen solid.

3 Remove the ice ring from the mould, place it in a plastic bag, and close it securely. Keep the ice ring in the freezer until you are ready to serve the punch. You may want to make two ice rings if you are serving a large group.

Snowball Cookies

These Christmas cookies will be a reminder of the snow-drifts around Green Gables.

1 cup	*butter, softened*	*250 mL*
½ cup	*powdered sugar*	*125 mL*
2 cups	*all-purpose flour*	*500 mL*
½ tsp	*salt*	*2 mL*
1 tsp	*chopped pecans or walnuts*	*5 mL*

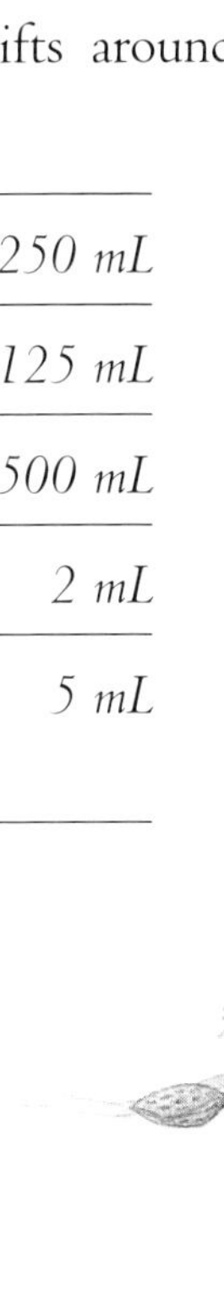

1 Preheat oven to 400°F (200°C).

2 Combine all the ingredients and roll dough into balls the size of a walnut. Place the cookies 1 inch (2.5 cm) apart on ungreased cookie sheets.

3 Bake for seven to eight minutes.

4 Roll the warm cookies in sifted powdered sugar; re-roll them in powdered sugar when they are cool, if necessary. Makes 4 dozen cookies.

Gingerbread Cookies

If you made cookies from the leftover dough of the Green Gables Gingerbread House (see page 32), serve a plateful of them to your guests.

A Green Gables Christmas Carolling Party

If a Christmas Concert is a bit too ambitious for you (after all, Christmas holidays now are more involved and busier than they were in Anne's day), why not invite a group of friends to go Christmas carolling one evening? This was a popular activity in Anne's day, too. In fact, carolling has been a popular part of Christmas celebrations for centuries in many parts of the world.

Go to several neighbourhood houses and sing a Christmas carol or two in front of each house, wish the family a "Merry Christmas" and move on to the next house. It might be a good idea to print the words to a few of the carols on a sheet of paper or make up a little booklet of carols so everyone will be singing the same words!

You may need flashlights to walk with and to read the words with. Anne and her friends would have used candles or lanterns, of course, since flashlights had not been invented. If you choose to have candles, you will certainly need to use a great deal of caution to keep hair and clothing away from the open flames. You will also want to make some bobèches (drip guards) to keep melting wax from dripping onto your gloves. These bobèches can also be used on table candles in candlesticks. Do not allow the candle flame to burn down too closely to the bobèches.

Wild-Rose Bobèches

For each Wild-Rose Bobèche, you will need:

2 pink index cards or other lightweight pastel pink card stock, 5 by 7 inches (13 by 18 cm)

Pencil

Scissors

Tall candles

1 Enlarge the diagram of a wild rose shown below and sketch it on one of the index cards. The finished outline should be 5 inches (13 cm) across.

2 Cut out the rose shape and the centre hole slits. Check to see that it fits the candle snugly. Use this cut-out as a template for the rest of bobèches you want to make.

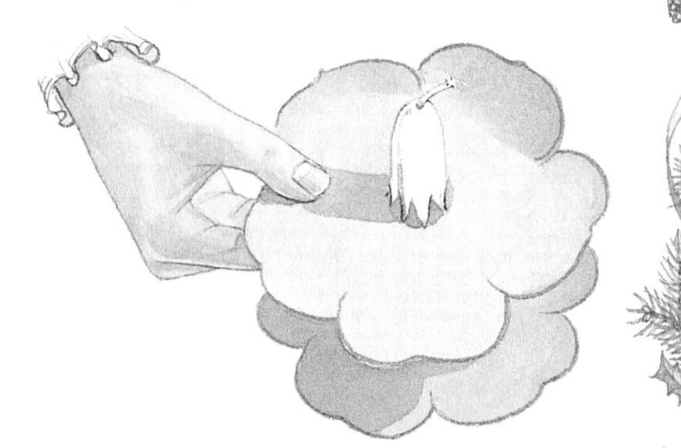

3 Use two rose cut-outs for each candle. Slide them onto the candle from the top so that the hole slits stand up around the candle. Bend the petals of the rose up slightly. The rose should rest on top of your fingers as you hold the candle.

Wild-Rose Petal Cups and Ice Cream

After the carolling, invite your friends in for refreshments—punch and cookies, as suggested for the Christmas Concert on page 77, or perhaps some hot cocoa to warm you up. For an extra-special treat, make some of these Wild-Rose Petal Cups for dessert.

For each cup you will need:

2 squares (2 ounces/60 g) white chocolate candy coating

Red food colouring

Waxed paper

1 Place the white chocolate in a small bowl, then put the bowl into a pan of barely simmering water. Stir gently to melt the chocolate. Remove a tablespoon (15 mL) or so of the melted chocolate to a small dish and add a drop or two of food colouring to it to tint it a rosy pink.

2 With a tablespoon, spread the white chocolate into petal shapes on the waxed paper. Make five large petals (about 3 inches long/7.5 cm), four medium petals (about 2 ½ inches /6 cm long), and four small petals (about 2 inches/5 cm long). Leave a small spoonful of the melted chocolate in the bowl for use in step 3. With a toothpick, swirl some of the pink chocolate mixture into each white petal.

3 When the petals are firm (they will set faster if you place them in the refrigerator), peel the petals from the waxed paper. Drop the spoonful of reserved melted chocolate (gently re-heated, if necessary) onto a small piece of waxed paper set on a saucer. Arrange the petals in the soft chocolate base starting with the largest petals on the outside and ending with the smallest petals on the inside. Leave a space in the middle for a scoop of ice cream.

4 To serve the Wild-Rose Petal Cup, carefully peel the waxed paper from the bottom of the finished cup and set the cup on a dessert plate. Place a scoop of vanilla or strawberry ice cream in the centre of the rose and serve immediately.

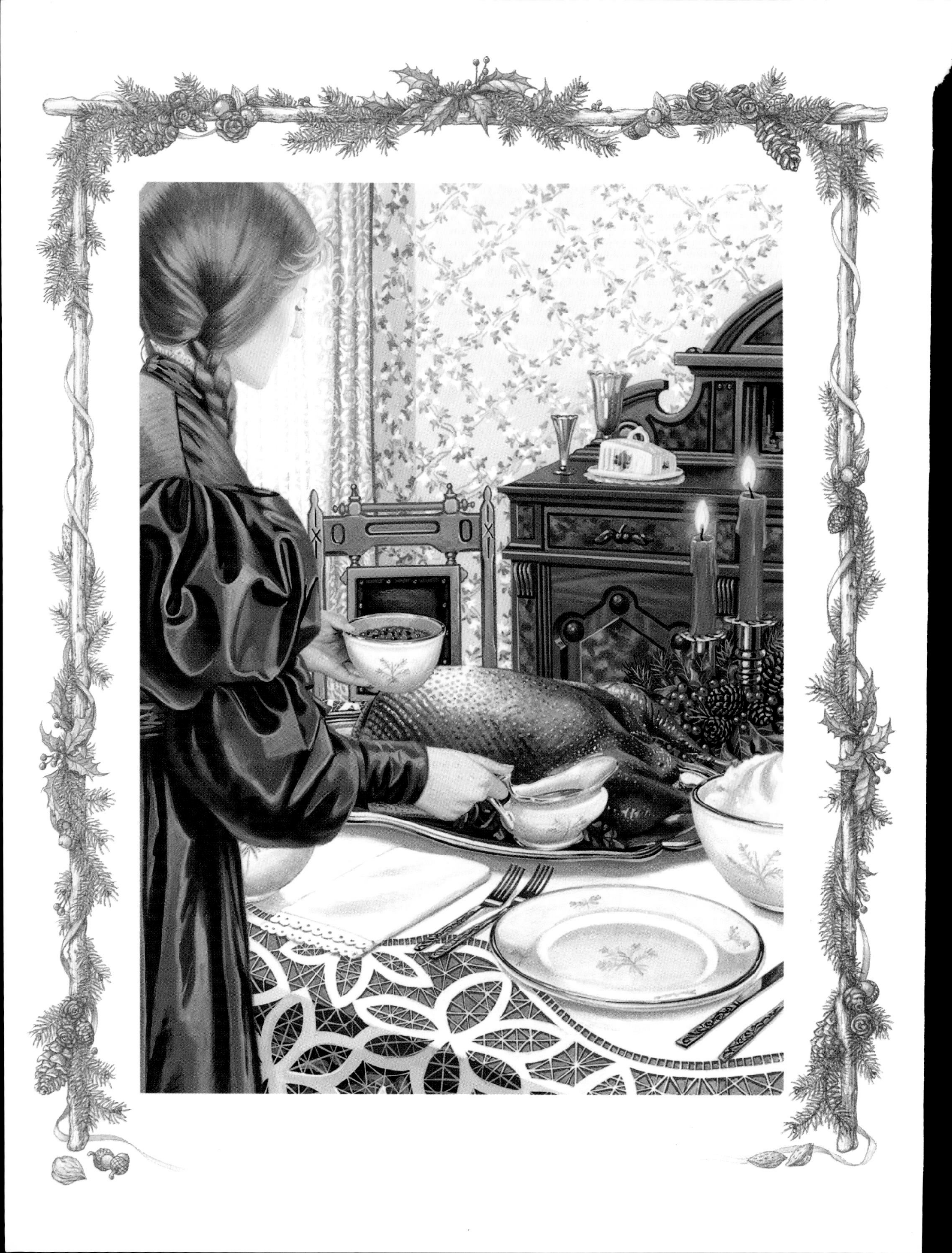

A Cosy Christmas Dinner at Green Gables

Merry was the feast and long; and when it was over they gathered around the cheer of the red hearth flame.

ANNE'S HOUSE OF DREAMS, XV

Only a few Christmas dinners are described in the Anne books and, since hardly any specific dishes are mentioned, we should assume that the Christmas feasts that were served at Green Gables, the House of Dreams and Ingleside followed the traditional menu found on most tables of the Victorian age. Nearly always included were turkey or goose, stuffing, gravy, rolls, vegetables, salads, cranberries, mince pies, fruit cake and, inevitably, plum pudding.

Having searched through the Anne books for special-occasion meals, including Christmas, and having checked old Prince Edward Island cookbooks for further information, we have chosen a Christmas menu that includes many of Anne's favourites and represents a typical holiday feast from Anne's day. (The recipes will serve six people.)

MENU

Anne's Cream of Onion Soup
Four Winds Roast Goose with "Prunes and Prisms" Stuffing
Green Gables Bread Sauce
Cranberry Relish
Island Whipped Potatoes
Anne's Glazed Carrots
Mrs. Lynde's Plum Pudding with Custard Sauce
Marilla's Ginger Tea

Anne's Cream of Onion Soup

This soup was one of Anne's favourites and she was rather proud of her ability to make it. She concocted it for a dinner in honour of a famous author, Mrs. Charlotte E. Morgan, who was coming to Green Gables.

ANNE OF AVONLEA, XVI

3 tbsp	*butter*	*45 mL*
2	*large onions, sliced*	*2*
¼ cup	*cornstarch*	*50 mL*
1 tbsp	*all-purpose flour*	*15 mL*
1 tsp	*salt*	*5 mL*
1 tsp	*white pepper*	*5 mL*
2 cups	*boiling water*	*500 mL*
4 cups	*milk, scalded*	*1 L*
1 cup	*mashed potatoes*	*250 mL*
2 tbsp	*chopped parsley, sliced green onions or chopped chives (optional)*	*25 mL*

1 Melt the butter in a large pot and add the sliced onions. Cook the onions over medium heat until they are lightly browned. Stir in the cornstarch, flour, salt and pepper and cook for a minute, until the cornstarch and flour are lightly browned. Gradually add the boiling water, stirring constantly. Continue cooking the mixture until it is smooth and slightly thickened.

2 Mix the scalded milk with the mashed potatoes and stir them into the onion mixture. Simmer the soup for a few minutes and serve it, as Anne said, "as soon as it's done."

3 Sprinkle each serving with chopped parsley, sliced green onions or chives, if you like.

Four Winds Roast Goose with "Prunes & Prisms" Stuffing

For Anne and Gilbert's first Christmas in their "House of Dreams," Anne roasted two geese to serve her guests. Marilla, who had never spent a Christmas away from Green Gables, Mrs. Rachel Lynde and twins Davy and Dora Keith had come sixty miles to Four Winds Harbour from Green Gables by train. Mrs. Cornelia Bryant and Captain Jim, who were Anne and Gilbert's neighbours at Four Winds Harbour, also came for dinner.

ANNE'S HOUSE OF DREAMS, XV

1	*8- to 10-pound (4- to 4.5-kg) goose, cleaned and washed in cold water*	*1*
1 tbsp	*orange juice*	*15 mL*
	Salt and pepper	
	Oil or melted butter	
	"Prunes and Prisms" stuffing (see page 88)	

1 Preheat the oven to 325°F (160°C).

2 Pat the goose dry, inside and out, with paper towels. Brush the inside cavities with orange juice. Sprinkle the inside of the goose liberally with salt and pepper. Spoon the stuffing mixture loosely into the large cavity first, then the smaller cavity if there is stuffing remaining.

3 Skewer the openings closed with metal skewers; tie the legs together with white string. Place the goose on a rack in a shallow roasting pan. Prick the skin of the goose all over with a fork, then brush it thoroughly with melted butter or oil.

4 Roast for two to three hours, basting the goose every fifteen or twenty minutes with the fat that has dripped into the roasting pan. Remove the extra fat with a spoon or a bulb baster and save it for making gravy or bread sauce if you like.

5 The goose is done when a meat thermometer inserted in the thigh of the bird registers 185°F (67°C). The juices of the thigh should run clear.

6 When the goose is done, remove it from the roasting pan and set it on a warm platter. Cover it lightly with aluminum foil and let it "rest" for about fifteen minutes before carving it. Serve the goose surrounded with its "Prunes and Prisms" Stuffing, along with Green Gables Bread Sauce (see page 89).

“Prunes and Prisms” Stuffing

Charles Dickens’s phrase “prunes and prisms” from his novel *Little Dorrit* was applied several times in the Anne books. It referred to prim and proper behaviour.

12	*large pitted prunes*	*12*
12	*whole dried apricots*	*12*
1 cup	*orange juice*	*250 mL*
3	*tart apples, peeled, cored, and cut in 1-inch (2.5-cm) chunks*	*3*
1	*onion, peeled and cut in 1-inch (2.5-cm) chunks*	*1*

1. Soak the prunes and apricots in the orange juice for about thirty minutes. Drain the fruit, discarding the juice, and mix the prunes, apricots, apples and onions together in a large bowl.

2. Stuff the goose just before roasting as directed above.

Green Gables Bread Sauce

Anne made a bread sauce (from Marilla's leftover homemade bread) to serve with the roosters she baked for Mrs. Charlotte E. Morgan. Bread sauce was often made in Anne's day instead of gravy.

2 tbsp	*butter (or goose fat)*	*25 mL*
1 cup	*stale breadcrumbs*	*250 mL*
1½ cups	*milk*	*375 mL*
	Salt and pepper to taste	

1 Melt 1 tbsp (15 mL) of the butter in a skillet. When the butter begins to sizzle, stir in ½ cup (125 mL) of the breadcrumbs. Cook over medium heat until they are nicely browned. Set aside.

2 In a small pot, heat the milk slowly until tiny bubbles form around the edges. Remove from heat before the milk boils up.

3 Put the remaining ½ cup (125 mL) of breadcrumbs in a heavy saucepan over medium heat and pour the scalded milk over them. Stir and simmer the mixture for about twenty minutes. Add remaining butter, salt and pepper. Keep the sauce warm until you are ready to serve it.

4 Pour the bread sauce over slices of roast goose and sprinkle the browned breadcrumbs on top, or serve the bread sauce topped with the browned breadcrumbs in a warm bowl and let each guest spoon the sauce over their slices of roast goose.

Makes about two cups.

Cranberry Relish

Cranberries have been a traditional part of Christmas dinner since the early settlers of North America discovered them growing in the bogs of New England. They add a dash of colour to the table and their sweet-tart flavour is delicious with roast turkey or goose.

1 lb	*fresh cranberries*	*500 g*
1	*large orange, peeled and seeded (reserve peel)*	*1*
3	*stalks celery*	*3*
1 cup	*walnuts*	*250 mL*
1½ cups	*sugar*	*375 mL*

1 Remove the inside white part of the orange rind and discard, saving the outside orange part.

2 Grind or finely chop the cranberries, orange and orange peel, celery and walnuts. Mix them all together in a large bowl and stir in the sugar. Cover the bowl and refrigerate the mixture for one or two days, stirring it occasionally.

3 Serve as a relish or on lettuce leaf cups, as a salad.

Island Whipped Potatoes

Prince Edward Island is famous for its delicious potatoes. Matthew, like most of the farmers on the Island, grew potatoes for export as well as enough to supply Green Gables each year. In winter, the potatoes typically would have been stored in the cellar, layered in fine, dry sand in large wooden barrels. Christmas dinner at Green Gables would not have been complete without a bowl piled high with snowy whipped potatoes.

6–8	*medium- to large-sized potatoes*	*6–8*
1½ tsp	*salt*	*7 mL*
2 cups	*milk*	*500 mL*
1 tbsp	*butter*	*15 mL*
	Salt and pepper to taste	
	Paprika (optional)	

1 Peel the potatoes, cut them into 1-inch (2.5-cm) chunks, and place the chunks in a large saucepan. Cover the potatoes with cold water, add the 1 ½ tsp (7 mL) of salt, and bring the water to a boil over high heat. Put a lid on the pot, and turn the heat down to simmer for about twenty minutes or until potatoes are tender. Lift the lid from time to time to keep the potatoes from boiling over and check to see if more water is needed.

2 Drain the potatoes through a colander (do be careful — the pot is heavy and hot!) and put them back into the dry pot. Cover the pot and let the potatoes stand in a warm place for about five minutes.

3 Meanwhile, heat the milk until it just begins to steam (do not let it boil) and add the butter.

4 Mash the potatoes with a fork or potato masher, or put them through a potato ricer if you have one. Make sure there are no lumps!

5 Beat the milk and butter into the potatoes (Anne and Marilla would have used a wooden spoon but you can use a mixer if you like) until they are nice and fluffy. Taste them to see if they need a little more salt and little pepper.

6 Pile the potatoes into a warm bowl, sprinkle them with red paprika for a festive touch, and serve them immediately.

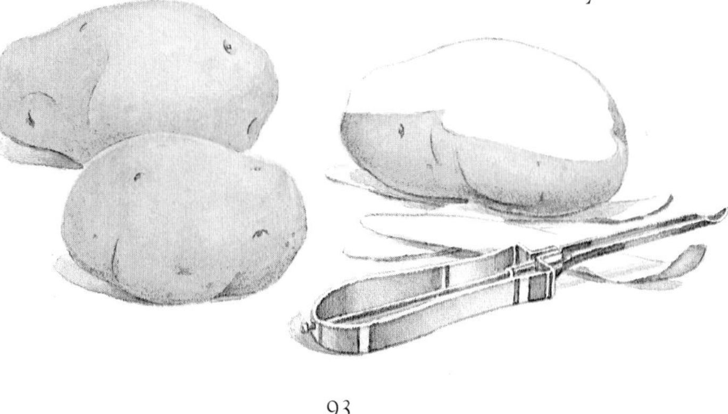

Anne's Glazed Carrots

"Carrots! Carrots!" Gilbert Blythe was determined to make Anne notice him on their first day of school together in Avonlea, but teasing her about her red hair turned out to be the worst way for him to gain her attention. At the time, Anne believed her red hair to be her worst feature and termed it her "lifelong sorrow." To punish Gilbert for his "mean, hateful" comment, Anne jumped up from her desk, cracked her slate over Gilbert's head, and did not speak to him for the next five years!

A platter of glistening glazed carrots will be yet another reminder of Anne on your Christmas table.

2 lb	*whole carrots*	*1 kg*
2 tsp	*salt*	*10 mL*
½ cup	*butter*	*125 mL*
½ cup	*brown sugar, packed*	*125 mL*
	Parsley (optional)	

1 Peel and trim off the ends of the carrots. Carefully cut them in half lengthwise. If the carrots are large, cut them into quarters. Place the carrots, along with the salt, in a large pan and cover them with water.

Bring water to a boil, then lower the heat and simmer the carrots until they are tender, about ten to fifteen minutes.

2 Drain the carrots, put them back in the pan and set the pan over low heat. Add the butter and when it has melted, sprinkle in the sugar. Toss the carrots in the butter/sugar mixture until they are well coated.

3 To serve the carrots, place them lengthwise and slightly overlapping on a large warm platter. A bunch of parsley at each end of the platter would make a nice garnish.

Mrs. Lynde's Plum Pudding with Custard Sauce

Plum pudding for Christmas was as popular in Canada and the United States in Anne's day as it was in Great Britain. Mrs. Rachel Lynde, Marilla's lifelong neighbour in Avonlea, brought "an enormous plum pudding" for the first Christmas dinner at Anne and Gilbert's "House of Dreams," thinking that "a college graduate of the younger generation" could not possibly know how to make a plum pudding "properly."

You may not need to make a pudding quite as "enormous" as Mrs. Lynde's. Here is a smaller version that will make six to eight servings; you can double it if you wish.

1½ cups	*raisins*	*375 mL*
1½ cups	*currants*	*375 mL*
1 cup	*beef suet, chopped fine (you may substitute lard if you prefer)*	*250 mL*
⅓ cup	*chopped candied orange peel*	*75 mL*
1½ cups	*all-purpose flour*	*375 mL*
1½ cups	*white breadcrumbs (not toasted)*	*375 mL*
1¼ cups	*sugar*	*300 mL*
1½ tsp	*ground cinnamon*	*7 mL*
1 tsp	*ground nutmeg*	*5 mL*
1 tsp	*ground mace*	*5 mL*
1 tsp	*salt*	*5 mL*
½ cup	*molasses*	*125 mL*
6	*eggs, well beaten*	6

1 Mix the raisins, currants, suet and candied orange peel in a large bowl. Add about ½ cup (125 mL) of the flour and toss the fruit in it until all pieces are coated lightly. Mix the rest of the flour with the breadcrumbs, sugar, spices and salt, pour it over the fruit, and mix well.

2 Stir the molasses into the beaten eggs and pour over the fruit mixture. Mix thoroughly and set aside.

There are several methods for cooking the pudding — steaming, boiling, or baking it in a water bath.

To steam the pudding:

1 Sprinkle a well-greased pudding mould generously with sugar, and fill it two-thirds full of batter. Cover the mould securely with its lid. If you do not have a pudding mould, you can use a metal bowl or large coffee can and fit several layers of aluminum foil tightly on top of the bowl as a cover. Tie the foil down securely with string.

2 Place the filled and covered mould on a rack in a large, heavy pan over medium heat. Add 1 inch (2.5 cm) of boiling water and cover the pan tightly. When the water boils, lower the heat

to simmering. Steam the pudding for five hours, adding water from time to time if necessary.

3 When the pudding is done, remove it from the hot water, uncover it, and let it cool for about ten minutes. Unmould it onto a platter and serve it with custard sauce.

To bake the pudding:

1 Prepare the mould and fill with batter as in the steaming instructions above.

2 Place the filled and covered mould in a roasting pan and put it in an oven preheated to 325°F (160°C). Pour boiling water into the roasting pan to a depth of 1 to 2 inches (2.5 to 5 cm). Bake the pudding for 3½ hours or until done. Add more water to the roasting pan as necessary. Uncover the mould during the last half-hour of baking.

3 Remove the pudding from the water bath, cool it for five minutes, and unmould it onto a plate or platter.

To boil the pudding:

1 Flour a large cloth and turn the pudding out of the bowl onto the centre of the cloth. Gather the cloth loosely around the pudding and tie it securely with heavy string, allowing some room for the pudding to expand during cooking.

2 Place the wrapped pudding in a large pot of boiling water (there should be enough water to cover the pudding) and simmer it for five hours, adding more hot water as needed to keep the pudding immersed.

3 When the pudding is cooked, remove it from the water and let it cool for about ten minutes. Unwrap the pudding, place it on a platter and serve it with custard sauce.

You can make the plum pudding well in advance of the day you want to serve it. Wrap it well and keep it refrigerated. Before serving, warm it in its mould over simmering water for about an hour.

It is traditional to top a plum pudding with a sprig of holly when it is served. For a dramatic presentation, ½ cup (125 mL) of warmed brandy is poured over the pudding and lit with a match so that the pudding is flaming when it is brought to the table — this rather daring flourish requires adult supervision.

Another custom is hiding charms or coins wrapped in paper or foil in the pudding. Ribbons are tied to the charms before they are inserted into the cooked pudding and the ends are allowed to trail down the sides of the pudding. Each diner removes a charm before eating the pudding. The pudding can then be flamed if desired.

Serve the plum pudding with Custard Sauce.

Custard Sauce

Surely Anne never served plum pudding with custard sauce without thinking of the time she forgot to cover a pitcherful of it in the Green Gables pantry with nearly disastrous results. Marilla was about to serve the leftover sauce, "warmed up," to guests when a horrified Anne shrieked, "Marilla, you mustn't use that pudding sauce. There was a mouse drowned in it. I forgot to tell you before."

Keep the sauce in the refrigerator — covered, of course! — until you are ready to serve it.

1 cup	*milk*	*250 mL*
1 cup	*cream*	*250 mL*
½ cup	*sugar*	*125 mL*
	Pinch of salt	
2	*eggs, well beaten*	2
½ tsp	*vanilla extract*	*2 mL*

1 Heat the milk and cream over low to medium heat in a heavy-bottomed pot until the mixture begins to steam; do not let it boil.

2 Add the sugar and salt to the beaten eggs and mix thoroughly. Pour a little of the hot milk into the eggs and stir, then pour the egg mixture back into the hot milk. Cook, stirring constantly, until the custard begins to thicken (it will coat a spoon nicely when it is done). Remove the custard from the heat and let it cool. Add the vanilla.

3 Chill the custard sauce until you are ready to serve it. Warm it gently, if you wish, to serve it with the plum pudding.

Marilla's Ginger Tea

A pot of hot tea was on the table with every meal at Green Gables. Marilla even liked to make ginger tea sometimes. This special-occasion version of ginger tea is full of spices and will be delicious with Christmas dinner.

1 quart	*boiling water*	*1 L*
6 tsp	*tea leaves or 6 tea bags*	*30 mL*
¼ cup	*sugar*	*50 mL*
1	*lemon, thinly sliced*	*1*
1	*orange, thinly sliced*	*1*
1	*cinnamon stick*	*1*
½ tsp	*cloves*	*2 mL*
½ tsp	*ground ginger*	*2 mL*
	Slices of lemon or orange for garnish	

1 Spoon the tea leaves into a large teapot or heatproof pitcher.

Pour the boiling water over the tea leaves, add the sugar, sliced lemons and oranges, and the spices. Cover the pot, and let it steep for five minutes. Strain the tea into a warm teapot and serve hot in teacups.

2 Garnish each teacup with floating slices of lemon or orange, studded around the edges with cloves, if you wish.